LEAF

AND THE SKY OF FIRE

BY JO MARSHALL

ILLUSTRATED BY D.W. MURRAY

ISBN: 145630092X
ISBN-13: 9781456300920

"As someone who has worked to both protect an endangered species and engage young people in the environmental issues that will shape their future, I've learned that education through entertainment is a powerful force for positive change.

Today's youth can be leaders tomorrow AND today if only they are given the tools to become aware, inspired, and engaged.

The Twig book series powerfully accomplishes each of these needs, all the while reaching young people on their level with fun, family-friendly entertainment.

I have no doubt that, thanks to this book series, countless children will develop a passion for our natural world and all living things that require it to survive.

And for each young person who becomes inspired to care for our shared environment, not only will we foster a more caring society in the future, we will create a new cohort of leaders who will be agents of change today."

D. Simon Jackson
Founder and Chairman, Spirit Bear Youth Coalition
Executive Producer, The Spirit Bear CGI Movie
www.spiritbearyouth.org

"This epic story tells a colorful tale of stick creatures that live in trees and protect forests against harmful organisms and issues associated with climate change. As a bark beetle biologist, I can relate to the difficulties in reducing tree mortality caused by bark beetles and invasive insects. Young readers interested in the natural world and preserving our forests will enjoy this engaging story."

Dr. Richard W. Hofstetter
Forest Entomology Professor
Northern Arizona University School of Forestry

"This book is a wonderful read. The story and artwork are impeccably crafted and weave a fascinating tale that will help introduce children to the magic and majesty of the natural world. Importantly, it imparts a strong appreciation of the intricacies and interactions that occur in nature. As a child, it was just such books that helped instill within me a desire to understand nature, and ultimately, to work in conservation. This book teaches in the best way possible – by igniting curiosity and building connections with the one thing that truly supports us all- our home, Earth."

Dr. Diana L. Six
Professor, Department of Ecosystem & Conservation
    Sciences
Integrated Forest Entomology/Pathology
University of Montana

"The environmental messages contained in this highly entertaining series of stories are certainly important and are told in a way that will engage children everywhere.

The educational value of these books cannot be underestimated especially at a time when we desperately need to create a culture that is committed to protecting our natural wonders."

Dr. David Edwards
Manager of Education
The British Columbia Wildlife Park

The Twig Stories Series

Twigs are adventurous stick creatures
who live in knotholes of ancient trees.

When climate changes threaten
even the smallest of creatures in their old forest,
Twigs fight back
and learn to stick together to survive!

Twig stories are environmental fantasies
with family values
for today's independent readers

A percentage of royalties are donated
to nonprofit organizations
concerned with protection of endangered wildlife,
nature conservancy,
and investigating climate change challenges.

More Twig stories by Jo Marshall

Leaf & the Rushing Waters

Leaf & the Long Ice

Leaf & Echo Peak

www.twigstories.com

Acknowledgements

My sweet daughter Ali made Twigs eternal with her enthusiastic, loving involvement in every detail. My sensible son, John, brought levity to my drama. My gratitude to David Murray whose exquisite art gave Leaf perfect expression. So much appreciation goes to Bridget Rongner and Ali Bloechl for their invaluable editing and extraordinary contributions. So many thanks to Tim, my brilliant yet practical husband. All my forest paths lead back to him.

LEAF AND THE SKY
OF FIRE

For Ali Jo

who gave me the best ideas

CHAPTER ONE

WHOSE HOME IS IT?

T ears stung her pale, gray eyes. Star watched her father tighten his shoulder strap, twist a braided rope around his waist, and carefully stuff poison darts in a pouch. At last he was ready to leave. He kissed Star's leafy, silvery hair. She bravely squared her shoulders. He tried to hug his pale, trembling son, but Moon angrily pushed him away, so sadly he turned to his father and gently squeezed his arm.

He whispered softly to the frail, old Twig, "You know what to do if I don't return."

Star's father left them. He disappeared among dying trees to join the others. Soon, stick creatures armed with darts, ropes, rocks, and whips moved stealthily beside him. They spoke only in murmurs. But the brittle needles revealed their wary steps. Wavy shadows gave them away. The deadly swarm gathered in the forest and surrounded them.

The North Twigs' fate was decided.

Very far away from the dying North Forest, an impish Old Seeder Twig practiced being invisible. His green, leafy hair blended with the leaves of the thin limb where he crouched. Stiff fronds sprouted at the limb's tip and hid his head. He narrowed his large, emerald-colored eyes, and curled his brown toes into grooves in the rough bark. The Old Seeder where he crouched was the tallest and oldest tree in the vast forest.

He was Leaf, a stick creature.

A large, roomy knothole in the massive, ancient tree was Leaf's home, his family's haven. Leaf felt smug. His Twig skills were excellent. If he stayed perfectly still, he looked just like the tree.

This is good, Leaf thought, *to hide so well*.

Leaf was ready to be a hunter in the forest. Yet, instead of hunting, he was stuck in his haven. He had to care for his tiny twin brothers, Buddy and Burba. His Mumma and Pappo had taken his little sister, Fern, to gather nuts and berries, and had left them here all morning. Leaf looked into the haven through its knothole-doorway and frowned. Taking care of his annoying twin brothers was Leaf's least favorite thing to do.

Buddy wasn't so bad. He was the calm one, with golden eyes and tiny, green, round sprouts that burst from his head. *But Burba* (who looked just like Buddy, except for his wild orange eyes) *is the worst Twig ever,* Leaf thought with dismay.

Leaf, sighed, stood up, and reluctantly stepped through the knothole into their large hollow. He leaned against the wall, crossed his arms, glowered at the twins playing on the floor, and sulked.

Feelers poked through a small, high knothole above Leaf's head, and disrupted his mood. The knobby hole had been left unplugged so that the sunbeams could stretch inside the haven, and the morning breeze could swirl around. A curious, orange-speckled stinkbug was exploring. Leaf stared dismally at the slowly creeping creature then scowled and waved his hands to shoo it away. The stinkbug hesitated for a moment then crawled all the way through the knothole and squatted on the wall. It rubbed its back legs together, rolled its bulgy, dark eyes then continued to scratch its way down the smooth wooden wall to the floor.

Buddy and Burba had been playing happily—making hand shadows with the sunbeams and swatting the gold dust billows. But now they giggled with delight as their bizarre, new guest refused to leave their home. The twins scooted closer to it. The glittery bug was nearly as large as they were, and certainly more interesting than dust billows. The twins were just asking for trouble.

"Watch out, it's a stinkbug!" warned Leaf. "Better leave it alone!"

"Better leave it alone, Burba!" repeated Buddy with his funny, garbled way of speaking. He rocked back and forth on his bottom, pulled his toes, and giggled good-naturedly.

Burba grinned mischievously, glanced at Leaf then back at the bug. The evil twin's eyes gleamed wickedly with joy. It was another wonderful opportunity to disobey his older brother.

"You're gonna be sorry!" warned Leaf. He glared at Burba.

Burba reached out his pudgy, short finger and poked the stinkbug right between its eyes. The bug's antennae circled feverishly. It spread its legs wide in a defensive stance, rolled its bulgy eyes furiously at Burba, and fluttered its stubby wings. Then it squatted lower and pressed its black belly against the floor to appear fat and even more alarming.

"Better stop now, Burba!" Leaf spoke with a low, menacing tone and cautiously stepped past the stinkbug to pull Burba away. "Stop!" he shouted.

Burba never stopped. He rarely obeyed his older Twig brother. Burba giggled, stuck out his hand, and wriggled his fingers in the stinkbug's face.

Leaf knew what would happen next.

The stinkbug lifted its pointy, black butt high up in the air and bounced it vigorously up and down. It spewed a foul-smelling, invisible spray. The twins shrieked in disgust at the horrible stink! Before the stench could completely blanket them, Leaf sprinted across the floor, swept up the two howling twins, and hurtled through the knothole. He paused on the porch-branch just outside to throw Burba on his back and Buddy on his hip.

"Hold on tight!" Leaf cried out.

They were very high. Their haven was halfway up the enormous cedar. Hastily, Burba scrambled onto Leaf's shoulders, perched on his head, and gripped his green leaves. Leaf held Buddy with one arm. That left him only one hand with which to climb down the tree. Buddy clung to Leaf's chest and squeezed his eyes shut. Heights frightened him.

After a brief, alarmed glimpse at the stinkbug which now aggressively crawled towards them, Leaf dove headlong through the Old Seeder's long limbs to the mossy forest floor below. Needles whipped past Leaf's head and stung his eyes, but he was able to skillfully catch limb after limb with only one hand as they fell toward the ground. Buddy moaned with fright at the speed with which they rushed through the tree. As they neared the roots, Leaf and the twins burst through a clump of fern-like fronds, tumbled off a low branch, and fortunately plopped right onto an oversized, white mushroom so that their clumsy landing was a soft one. Burba's fists had been clenched so tightly to Leaf's leafy head the whole way down, he managed to yank out a few of Leaf's bright green leaves.

Irritated, Leaf tossed Burba onto the moss. He then gently sat Buddy on a small mushroom.

The stinkbug's perfume curled its way out the knot-hole, over the broad branch just beyond, and around the pretty green sprays of needles. Slowly it fell down through the unsuspecting limbs of the towering tree. Stealthily, one by one, the stink chased away the blue jays, chickadees, nuthatches, grosbeaks, towhees, and finally the squirrels.

"*Screee! Screee!*" screamed a red-headed wood-pecker as the sickly smell suffocated the tree's bark. At once, it flapped its wings frantically against the trunk to get away, but instead flew into a clump of needles.

Its black-speckled feathers exploded in all directions. "*Screee!*" it shrieked angrily at the rude bug.

The stinkbug crawled happily to the knothole and peeked out. It waved its long antennae in slow spirals, scratched itself with its bristly legs, and planted itself snugly in the doorway. Pleased with the commotion it had created in the Old Seeder, it squatted and smirked.

Burba and Buddy giggled with delight.

"Great, Burba! Just great!" exclaimed Leaf. He gazed up through the branches at the stinkbug, which now occupied their haven. "Wait until Pappo and Mumma get back from hunting! They'll really be happy! They'll have to get the stinkbug out of the knothole and the stink out of our haven!"

The twins stopped giggling immediately. They glanced uneasily at each other.

Just as if they heard their names mentioned, Pappo and Mumma pushed through a huckleberry bush not very far away. Cheerfully, Pappo stepped toward Leaf, paused, and looked back over his shoulder with an expression of happy expectation. His wispy, white leaves barely covered his head but his golden eyes twinkled with youthful delight. Mumma followed a little more slowly, still limping from her terrible fall the season before. As usual, her golden leaves were tied into a tight knot on top of her head. Her eyes burned bright with the orange and amber colors of autumn.

From the thick bush behind them, the sloppy, golden leaves of Fern's tousled hair popped out. She walked backwards, tugged at a large stuffed moss bag, and tried to free it from the tangles. Fern turned, smiled broadly, brushed her unkempt, leafy hair from her eyes, and announced, "Not bad for my first outing, eh?" Proudly, she patted the stuffed moss bag, and blinked her happy, orange eyes.

Mumma and Pappo turned to Leaf and laughed. "She is a great hunter!" exclaimed Pappo. "You should have seen her, Leaf!"

"She's the most eager hunter I've seen!" praised Mumma and gave Fern a warm look.

Pappo added, "She wanted to bring home every cappynut, berry, and seed she could find. I was so surprised! She actually brought back more on her first gathering than you did, Leaf!"

Fern puffed up her chest and squared her shoulders, very proud. She gazed expectantly at Leaf. It was his turn to compliment her. She waited. But Leaf didn't move or speak. Fern was immediately irritated with his silence. He said nothing at all!

Fern taunted her older brother, "What's the matter, Leaf? Jealous?" But Leaf didn't look jealous. In fact, he looked grim.

Leaf pointed up. "A stinkbug's in the haven," he stated flatly.

Startled, Mumma, Pappo, and Fern jerked their eyes up to their haven's knothole far above. The black stinkbug still squatted in the knothole. It rolled its shimmering, bulgy eyes around, happy and content. At that same moment, its sickening stench finally rolled off the limbs directly above their upturned faces.

Leaf had had enough. Immediately, he scooped up Buddy and Burba, dove into the huckleberry bush, and yelled back, "Run for it!"

Pappo and Mumma abruptly followed Leaf.

Fern hesitated. One hand stubbornly gripped her treasures while the other waved furiously under her nose. Then finally, reluctantly, she abandoned the fat bundle and bolted into the bush too.

The Twigs crowded together amid the sweet-smelling leaves and plump berries of the huckleberry bush. They stared out through the thick brambles as if some horrible beast paced back and forth, ready to pounce on them. Suddenly, they all laughed—except Leaf.

"Now what?" asked Pappo. "I wonder how long the stinkbug plans to visit."

Leaf was completely disheartened. He should have forced the stinkbug to leave or stopped Burba before he poked it. Now he wondered if they would sit in the huckleberry bush all day.

"Well, let's not be so sad about it!" Mumma exclaimed. "Let's picnic at the creek!"

At once, the young Twigs tumbled out of the bush, raced along a shadowy trail, and slid down a mossy embankment to a cold, clear stream just deep enough for playful Twigs to stand knee-deep and splash each other.

Mumma leaned on Pappo as the two followed happily, and much more slowly, after them. Since the fall from the cherry blossom tree, Mumma often crept along like a slug—steady and sure, unhurried. Pappo patted her hand as they walked on the faint forest path, and she smiled sweetly at him.

The stinkbug stayed all day.

CHAPTER TWO

MOOK OF THE NORTH

The creek splashed a merry melody to the Twigs. Fern and Leaf scooped up cool water in cappynut shells and tossed it at the twins as they giggled, ran off, and hid. The morning blossoms drooped in the afternoon heat. The brilliant butterflies floated on silent wings amid bushes with leaves glowing like emeralds in the sun. Sunbeams danced with pollen dust in the air. Pappo threw his and Mumma's long, braided ropes over a low-hanging limb of a cherry tree and fashioned two swing-cradles for the twins. It was so lovely and lazy, Leaf half-wished the stinkbug would invade their haven every day.

Fern created tiny, stick Twig dolls for the twins. Burba watched intently as Fern pushed one thin stick through another for arms, stuck on green leaves for hair with a muddy paste, and then bent another smooth, flexible stick though the tangle for shaky legs. She mashed up the toes to be very curly—like teeny roots. She even twisted a thin vine over the shoulders and around the waist to look like the rope which Twigs always carried. She stuck a strong, long stem across the back to be the hunting tool. The stem resembled the strong walking stick, called a saver, which Twigs carried. She made a doll-Twig for Burba first, then another for Buddy. The twins carried their little dolls with them everywhere in the glade. As Leaf lay down in the shade, the twins bathed their new toys in the creek and giggled with delight as the teeny Twig-dolls floated along, rolling over and over in the slow, swirling currents.

Leaf felt sleepy. He lay back on the warm moss in the roots of the cherry tree, breathed in the rich scents, and napped. In his dream, he rode his sweet, speckled chipmunk named Whisper through the forest. Her whiskers and nose twitched from the pollen. Her curly, bushy tail was held high and her spotted back gleamed in the sun. He rode to a strange, rocky place. The hillside was full of dark caves. He slid from Whisper's back and she suddenly disappeared. Worried, he looked for her. Then he saw a frightening hole fall away into the hill before him. He pulled his saver from its loop on his back and held it across his chest to defend himself. He felt a creeping terror lurking in the cave. Leaf felt cold and afraid, yet took a deep breath and shoved his saver into the hard earth. With the clear stone at the top of the saver, he caught a bright sunray and directed its piercing beam into the deep black cavern. He peered over the dark edge. Far below, he saw stars—drifting stars—that glimmered in the dark shadows. There were so many. As he stared at them, an uneasy realization grew. They were not stars! They were eyes! Silvery eyes stared up. Huge eyes pleaded for help! Horrified, he saw they were the eyes of Twigs! Twigs were trapped deep within the cave!

Leaf struggled to wake up. He felt groggy and strangely cold. He shivered and shook his leafy head. For a moment he was uncertain where he was. Was it just a nightmare? How horrible it was! Before he could make sense of the dream, sharp, urgent cries startled him fully awake.

"Buddy! Burba!" Pappo yelled at the top of his voice.

Leaf saw Mumma and Fern jump quickly to their feet.

Pappo's voice was greatly concerned. "Buddy! Burba!"

Mumma and Fern shouted anxiously and searched for the twins in nearby bushes. Leaf sprang up and joined in the hunt. Walking in ever larger circles, they pushed apart glossy leaves and peered deep into the bushes. They searched the lush ferns and tangled tree roots. They peeked anxiously behind moss-covered rocks and under mushrooms. The twins could not be found.

Are they only hiding to play? Leaf wondered. *Only teasing us? No.* Leaf shook his head. *It is far too quiet for a game. They would have popped out giggling by now.*

Leaf slid down the creek bank. He found the stick dolls abandoned just before the stream plunged into a dark, leafy tunnel. Leaf bent down to look into the shadowy hole and saw a small circle of light far down at the other end. At once, he crouched low and quickly waded into the tunnel. Had the twins gone exploring here? Leaf worried at the disturbing idea. It was very dark, the water ran swiftly, and dangerous creatures hid in these slimy places.

A grating *oock!* startled Leaf. A burping, green-spotted, goliath frog guarded his mud pile. Its eyes glistened. Its tongue licked its wide mouth as it sat on top of the muck, waiting for a gnat to fly by. Leaf frowned and carefully circled around the slimy frog. He didn't want to dodge a long, sticky tongue just now. In these shadows, he could easily be mistaken for a praying mantis or some other tasty frog treat! Leaf examined the frog's belly to be sure it had not swallowed the twins. Were they stuck inside, kicking around and struggling? He saw only its sagging belly. The giant frog had not eaten for a while. Relieved, Leaf splashed on.

When Leaf reached the end of the tunnel he was blinded for a moment by the streaming sunlight. His eyes soon adjusted and he looked out at a wide clearing. A few willowy trees brushed against the edge of a grassy meadow. White, fluttering butterflies zigzagged above blue blossoms. Leaf knew the twins loved to chase butterflies. He wondered if they chased one here. Leaf crouched instinctively in the shadow of the tunnel and searched the open skies for danger. Hawks hunted from the sky. Their sharp eyes quickly spotted their prey and in an instant they would dive. Twigs were good to stuff in their nests, and the nests were usually built in the highest limbs of the tallest trees. Once stuffed in one, it was difficult for a Twig to escape. Leaf scanned the sky but saw no danger.

Then he heard giggling. The twins were here! But where? Across the meadow, Leaf saw a holly bush rustle and shake. A tiny porcupine baby popped out of the glossy leaves. Then Leaf heard more giggling. With a sigh, Leaf knew at once that the twins were chasing the poor harmless creature out of the holly bush.

The porcupine waddled hastily into the clearing, stumbled in the moss as it tried to stop, defiantly looked over its shoulder, rustled its stubby quills, and squeaked a warning to the twins. It sniffed the air with its pointy nose. Anxiously, it wrung its gray hands together. The spikes on its back swished back and forth, ruffled and stiff, as if ready to pierce the Twigs. At least the twins knew enough to stay far away. Finally the porcupine shuffled toward the roots of a cappy-nut tree where it could hide from the annoying Twig babes.

Across the meadow from Leaf, Buddy and Burba rolled out from the holly bush. They were still quite a distance from Leaf but saw him at once, yet they completely ignored him. Leaf stood with his hands on his hips—clearly annoyed. Buddy and Burba simply wrestled each other in the grass and pretended not to see him glowering at them.

Without any warning, a dark shadow swiftly passed over the meadow.

"Hide!" screamed Leaf. "Buddy! Burba! Hide in the bush!" Knowing terrible danger arrives from the sky, Leaf raced frantically toward the twins, but still they wrestled each other and ignored Leaf's shouts.

The shadow raced faster, grew larger, and finally smothered the tiny Twigs. A strange, high-pitched gurgling noise burst out just as Leaf launched himself through the air with all his strength. He nearly flew all the way to the twins. He skidded hard on his elbows, caught the twins in his arms, and hugged them tight. They all slid into the twisted thicket of the holly bush.

The twins finally realized they were in danger and lay silent. Frightened, they held their breath and tucked their heads under Leaf's arms. Leaf dared not move. He wondered if the hunter believed it had missed its prey and had flown away. All he knew for sure was that he and the twins must be silent and invisible.

Leaf heard a thump on the ground. His heart sank with fear for his little brothers. Would the hunter come for them in the roots? He wondered anxiously if he could carry both tiny twins and still run fast enough to get away. He simply must flee, he decided. He crushed

Buddy and Burba against his chest and raised himself up on one knee, ready to dash from the tangled bush and into the nearby forest.

Then he heard a reedy gurgling noise as if a wounded creature choked on its own breath. An odd voice cried out, "Sorry! Sorry! So sorry!"

Leaf carefully turned his head to peek out between the prickly brambles. All he could see was a tooler strutting about the clearing. A tooler did not hunt. It was only a silly bird known only for its merry whistle! It lived in thorny bushes, not trees, and was harmless. The tooler's feathers flashed and shimmered blue-green. Toolers only whistle but that was a voice he heard. *Could a tooler speak?*

Leaf studied the busy creature.

Curiously, a gold braid hung from his neck and dragged between his scaly legs upon the ground. The tooler briskly fluffed out his glowing feathers then marched back and forth as if the clearing belonged to him. The ridiculous bird jabbed his long, yellow beak viciously into the earth and yanked out a fat worm. Then he beat the struggling worm on a rock until it was stunned senseless. Satisfied he had beaten it to death, the tooler greedily gulped it down with one swallow. At once he searched for more worms, each time stabbing the earth brutally with his spear-like beak.

Maybe we disturbed his nest, Leaf considered. *Perhaps he lives here.* Leaf knew a tooler's nature was very far from that of a hawk and most likely meant no harm. Leaf relaxed.

"Sorry! Sorry!" the scratchy, choking voice cried out and coughed.

It was only then Leaf saw the crooked figure of a Twig kneeling in the tall grass. He had the knobby, gnarled knees and crooked hands of a very old Twig. He leaned over as if he was sick or injured. The elderly Twig fell back, sat on the ground, held his head between his knees, and rocked back and forth. He spoke to the earth.

"Sorry! Meant no harm! Was Pesky's fault! Stupid tooler never could stop fast enough!" The odd Twig sat and swayed as if off balance. He pressed his head tightly as if it might fall off his shoulders.

The tooler ignored him as he flipped over a flat rock, found a long purple worm, whacked it on the rock to stun it, and then instantly gulped it down.

Leaf whispered to Buddy and Burba, "Stay here! Be quiet!" and frowned at them to be sure they would. They bobbed their tiny heads in unison.

Leaf crawled out from the safety of the bush. Concerned about the weak old Twig, he stood wondering what to do.

Just then Pesky hopped over and with his sharp beak gently stroked the leafy white hair on the sick Twig's head as if trying to soothe him.

Leaf realized there was a strong bond between the two.

Quickly giving up the effort to comfort his friend, Pesky stepped away from the sad-looking Twig, flapped his wings, and rustled his feathers to shake out the dust.

Leaf eyed the bizarre bird. *What a weird tooler!* Even though the tooler had just eaten two worms, he now slung a fat beetle into the air, ripped it apart, and gulped it down just as if he were starving! But even so greedy, Leaf noticed that Pesky never strayed far from his sick companion. Leaf worried what it might do if he stepped too near, especially if Pesky were protective of the old Twig. But it was obvious the sick Twig needed help. Leaf knew he must do something.

"Oh, allo," said the wrinkly Twig. He had finally noticed Leaf. In a thin, gurgling voice he said, "Glad we found you! We've flown from the Land of the Dancing Sky Lights!"

Although Leaf didn't understand what the Twig was talking about, he answered him anyway, "Allo! I'm Leaf of the Old Seeder Twigs."

Just then, Pappo, Mumma, and Fern burst through the tunnel and into the sunny clearing. Completely ignoring the startled tooler and strange old Twig, they cried, "Did you find them? Leaf, are they here?"

Unable to wait in the brambles any longer, Buddy and Burba tumbled out and jumped into Mumma and Pappo's arms. Both twins' budding heads were smothered with kisses, hugs, and tears from Mumma, Pappo, and Fern.

"So sorry! So sorry!" the odd Twig gurgled again. "Didn't mean to scare you!"

Mumma, Pappo, and Fern had huddled protectively around the twins, but now they peeked through their tangled arms and, astonished, stared at the strange Twig.

The old Twig tried to politely stand up. He stated weakly, "I'm Mook. North Twig. Flew on Pesky. Need help. Twig babes all alone! Need help! Star. Moon. Help!" After this garbled and confusing rush of words, Mook promptly sank to the ground and fainted.

At once, Mumma limped over to Mook. From her belt, she took a cappynut shell which was full of water. She dribbled a few cool, wet drops onto the droopy leaves on Mook's head. She patted his crooked hands. Pappo grabbed a broad fern and fanned Mook's wrinkled face.

Fern, Buddy, and Burba were unconcerned about the sick, old Twig. Instead, they were fascinated by the tooler. They circled Pesky curiously and studied the tooler closely. Slowly, they reached out to try and touch his brilliant, luminescent feathers. They knew they should be very cautious. Birds often stuffed Twigs in their nests for bedding. But this tooler eyed them back with a curious expression and warm, soft eyes. He dipped his head so the young Twigs could stroke his neck and smooth, yellow beak.

Then Pesky whistled!

Surprised, the Twig twins stumbled backward, and Fern crouched instinctively.

Pesky gingerly stepped right over the tiny twins and Fern to Mook. He insistently nudged Mook's limp body and whistled softly in the twisted ear of the unconscious old Twig. Leaf realized Mook must faint a lot because Pesky seemed to know just what needed to be done and, indeed, it worked.

Mook moaned a little and sat up slowly. "Sorry! Not well. Am I here?"

Pappo and Mumma exchanged worried glances. This frail old Twig needed much care. Pappo looked up and searched the sky for danger. They needed to get out of the clearing.

"Leaf," said Pappo, "you and I will help Mook to our haven. The rest of you go home and prepare a bed and mint tea for him. We'll be there soon. Now go at once!"

Mumma and Fern nodded. Each took one of the twin's hands and led them away from the friendly tooler. Together, they walked back through the tunnel and waded up the creek.

Pappo and Leaf gently placed Mook's arms over their shoulders. They moved slowly and carried Mook securely between them in an arm cradle. Carefully, they splashed into the cool, dark tunnel. The slimy, goliath frog still guarded its mud pile. But seeing so many Twigs enter at once, it decided to hurry away. It splashed clumsily into the stream and only its bulgy, wet eyes could be seen floating just above the water.

Pesky was suspicious of the dark tunnel. He flapped his wings and took a running leap into the sky. For a moment, he hovered awkwardly above the three slow-moving Twigs as they entered the dark hole. Then the tooler clumsily spiraled higher and watched closely as Mook, Leaf, and Pappo disappeared. After a while, the three Twigs re-emerged from the other end of the tunnel, climbed carefully up the creek's bank, and gingerly stepped along shadowy paths toward the Old Seeder. Mook continually groaned and muttered, but Leaf and Pappo could not understand his words. They simply murmured soothingly in reply.

Pesky kept a wary eye on his dear friend as Pappo and Leaf carried him up the massive trunk of the Old Seeder and into their haven. Then the tooler landed just outside the round door of their knothole, peered through its small window, and studied the scene inside intently. Pesky knew Mook was in loving hands, so he turned away to search the deeply furrowed red bark for fat bugs. There were many juicy ones in the Old Seeder.

Inside, Pappo laid Mook on a moss bed in Leaf's small hollow. He stepped quietly over to Leaf and Mumma who waited beside the door in the larger hollow. He shook his head sadly.

"Is he going to be all right?" Leaf asked.

"There's no telling," Pappo said. "He's very ill. He mutters all the time, but he makes no sense at all." He

TWIG STORIES

shook his head and shrugged. "How's that tooler doing? Did he leave?"

Leaf looked out of the knothole to check on Pesky. "No, he's still here. He's stuffing himself!" Leaf answered with a grin. "He acts like he hasn't eaten in a season!" Leaf watched the busy tooler hop around with a caterpillar squirming wildly in his mouth.

Pesky glanced at Leaf. He hopped near the knothole, dipped his head as if in a friendly greeting then instantly glared angrily at the young Twig.

Startled, Leaf realized Pesky was warning him: Be careful with my Mook!

CHAPTER THREE

WHO LIVES IN A CAVE?

Giggles echoed in the musty cavern where they hid in the North Forest far from the Old Seeder.

"Quick! She's coming! Hide!"

Six tiny stick bodies tumbled over one another in a rush to find a shadow, a hollow, or a curve along the smooth granite wall in which to disappear. They pushed, tugged, and scrambled with each other over the few places to hide until one tiny voice piped up, "Act like trees!"

"Yes! Yes! Act like trees!" they whispered eagerly. Immediately, the tiny Twig babes struck crooked poses. Their hands and arms stuck out like twisted limbs of ancient trees. Their toes curled up on the clay earth like roots. Their faces froze, their eyes wide, not blinking. Still, it was difficult to control the giggles.

A young, slender Twig moved from the shadows and slowly stepped among the six Twig babes. With a surprised expression, she searched the air above their leafy heads. She moved slowly and spoke in a soft, wondering voice, "Where are the babes? Where did the babes go?"

Tiny giggles erupted.

"I thought they were here, but where have they gone? How did all of these trees grow in our cave so fast?" she asked, puzzled.

The babes could no longer tease the playful, loving Twig.

"Here we are!" delighted voices burst out. More giggles echoed in the cave.

"Oh!" said Star. "Thank the moon! What excellent trees you were! I thought a forest sprouted in our cave!" The babes gathered around her and tugged at her gentle hands.

"We were hiding! We were trees and you didn't see us!" explained one very tiny Twig with eyes like the bright blue sky. She stood on Star's toes and held onto her knees.

"Yes, you were amazing, Breeze!" acknowledged Star. "I looked for you, but I couldn't find you!" She clapped her hands lightly. "Playtime's over. Now it's story time!"

The babes giggled, tumbled, and rolled around on the clay floor, then finally settled down in a small circle around Star. She sat patiently waiting, perched on a slightly raised flat rock in their midst.

"Where's PapaMook?" asked Sand, a tiny, delicate Twig with huge, brown eyes and dust-colored buds sprouting from her head. Her wide, wondering eyes blinked quizzically at Star.

The Twigs babes all stared at Star. Their eyes asked the same question. Absentmindedly, Star traced a tree in the clay earth.

"Where's PapaMook? Where's PapaMook? Where's PapaMook?" they chanted.

Star raised a slender hand and patted the air to calm their voices. "Now, now," she soothed them sweetly, "I've told you over and over where PapaMook went."

"Tell us again! Tell us again!" they pleaded and scooted closer.

"All right, all right," Star waved both hands to silence them. Her eyes shone silver and flashed when upset. Her leafy hair curled up tight in silvery bundles—except for a few stray strands that hung to her shoulders—like tips of moonlit waves blown by a swirling wind. She cared for the six babes as if they were her own little sisters and brothers. In a way, they were. Now they had only her and her brother, Moon, to care for them.

Breeze, the very youngest, still wobbled on her chunky stick legs. Her blue eyes were brilliant and startling. Her white, curly hair sprouted with blue tips. Moss snuggled up next to Breeze. Naturally, Moss had dark green buds for hair and oval-shaped, golden eyes. Cone and Mist were inseparable. Cone's dark, glossy hair and deep black eyes were the opposite of Mist's limp, light gray hair and diamond eyes.

Then there was Pool. Star wondered what to make of Pool. With his white hair and silver eyes, he most resembled Star and her brother, yet they were not related, not in the same Twig branch at all. Barely older than the rest, Pool liked to pretend he wasn't part of the group. He was irritatingly stubborn. He enjoyed devising ways to annoy the other babes. He tossed tiny pebbles at them or blew dust in their eyes. He smirked whenever they looked at him angrily. Finally, they would simply turn their backs and ignore Pool. All the Twig babes played happily with whatever they could find in the cave—like pebbles, clay, cones, and sometimes hard red berries too old to eat. But Pool, well, Pool only stirred up trouble. Star sighed.

Star loved them all, but it was Sand who tugged at her heart the most. It was Sand who crawled into her lap now to hear the story of PapaMook once more. Sand curled her tiny fingers around Star's and looked up expectantly. Pool lay flat on his back and pushed the clay into clumps with his heels. He pretended not to listen.

Star waved her graceful hands to quiet the babes. She spoke with a soft, chirping voice, and although her eyes seemed sad, her tone was light and cheery. Star's voice fluttered against the cave walls like a trapped swallow seeking a way out.

She began, "PapaMook has flown away on Pesky. He's looking for the South Forest Twigs. When he finds them, they will all come back and help us move to a new tree home." Star paused. She knew what would happen next.

"Tell us about the forest! Tell us about the forest!" the Twig babes cried out at once.

Star cradled Sand and slid from the rock to sit on the clay earth. She crossed her legs and motioned for the babes to scrunch up closer to her. With a secretive whisper, she responded, "In the South Forest, the trees are tall and magnificent and they spread out in all directions as far as you can see. There is clear running water. Forest creatures live everywhere you look. There are havens up in tall trees that are warm, safe, and welcome Twigs to their knotholes. And best of all . . ." She waited as the babes held their breath. "And best of all...all the trees are green!"

"Oh!" the tiny Twigs exhaled together in wonder. "They're not brown?"

"No!" asserted Star firmly. "They're all green! Their fronds are soft, and they smell wonderful! There are no dead, brown needles surrounding them on the ground either! And do you know what else isn't in the South Forest?" Star dropped her voice to an even lower whisper. "There are no barkbiters!" A shiver ran through the tiny Twigs. They sat silent and still, trying to imagine a world without the gruesome barkbiters.

"Now," Star clapped her hands to change the dreary mood. "Let's all draw creatures in the dirt. I'll guess what they are, so draw them well!"

Even Pool enjoyed drawing. Star handed them their drawing sticks. The babes spread out, lay flat on the ground, and concentrated on scratching creatures in the clay. As she watched them, Star's thoughts wandered and, once again, drifted to the sad events which led them to this cave.

Long ago, their forest was emerald green, not brown. When Star's mother and father were young Twig babes, a terrible change began. Slowly and methodically, ravenous barkbiters crept into the forest and devoured one tree after another. First, they ate the only the weaker trees inside out, leaving them to rot only when the brittle branches of the dead trees crashed on the ground. But as their numbers grew, the barkbiters attacked the larger, healthier pine trees. They chewed their way into the center of the thick trunks. From center to bark, from root to tip, they gnawed, leaving horrible deep scars, until the magnificent trees' limbs drooped with the weight of their own dying fronds.

The Twigs of the North Forest knew the freezing ice of the cold season would destroy barkbiters, so they waited and did nothing to save the trees. But as seasons passed and the cold seasons came and went, the Twigs realized the seasons were not as cold as they used to be. The barkbiters and their eggs did not freeze. Many cold seasons passed but the barkbiters survived buried deep in the trunks of the infested trees. The beautiful trees in the Land of Dancing Sky Lights became brown and brittle.

It was then that the swarm of barkbiters struck the Twigs. One day in the forest, Star's mother and many other Twigs were suddenly attacked. Horrified, her father pleaded with all of the Twig branches of the North Forest to seek out the barkbiters and destroy them. But it was already too late. Merciless hordes of barkbiters overwhelmed the Twigs, the only creatures who might have been able to stop their ravenous rampage.

And there were so few places to escape.

After Star's father left them, PapaMook brought Star, Moon, and the babes to this cave. Then he flew away on Pesky to find help. Unfortunately, the bizarre tooler only allowed Mook on his back and viciously stabbed any other Twig who tried to ride him. Star, Moon, and the babes had no choice but to stay and wait for rescue.

The poor little Twig babes had sprouted in a dangerously wicked world. Their North Forest was dying, full of evil barkbiters, yet they were still just babes, and they giggled every day, except for Pool.

Star watched the babes draw their funny creatures in the clay. "We are lucky," she said to them, tucking away her grim memories. "We have a lovely, safe cave to live in. The stickytoes and looksalot guard us all the time."

Star waved her arm at the bright circle of light shining across from where they sat. The entrance was covered with thick, sticky webs that diffused the sunbeams. A large, dark shadow moved in front of the light. He had a long tail spiraled into a tight coil. A thin fin ran down his back, and broad, wavy stripes—blue and gold—circled his green body. He swayed back and forth, balanced on his odd two-toed hands and feet. The babes' eyes twinkled as they watched the wierd, painfully slow movements of the looksalot, so out of place in the North Forest.

"Is he going to walk now?" Breeze gurgled in anticipation.

The other babes giggled at the thought. The looksalot stepped incredibly slowly, placing each hand and foot as if he stepped on prickly seedpods. His bulging eyes rolled around constantly and stared in different directions at the same time. The looksalot was fascinating to watch when he walked—or whenever he moved at all.

"Not now, Breeze," Star answered. "He'll stay there. He's on guard!"

"Is he waiting for PapaMook to come?" Cone wondered.

Star said firmly, "PapaMook will come soon enough! Then we'll all take a trip to the green forest!" Star clapped her hands loudly, and in a no-nonsense voice said, "Now it's time to take a nap! Off you go!" Star stood up to emphasize her words. The babes moaned in unison but obediently shuffled away to curl up in their moss beds which were lined up along the far wall of the cave and tucked into brown shadows.

A slender figure, slightly taller than Star, stepped to her side from where he had been listening to the merry chatter. He said wryly, "So I guess you're not going to tell them how their mums and paps ended their lives fighting the barkbiters then?" It was Star's younger brother, Moon. Lately, his voice sounded only sour and bitter. He kicked a pebble at her to demonstrate his dissatisfaction with her optimistic storytelling.

Star briskly sidestepped the rolling stone and answered quietly, "What good would it do now? They're only babes. They don't even remember them, Moon!" Star sounded exasperated. She brushed back her feathery, silver leaves from her face.

Irritated with her, Moon shook his droopy, colorless leaves over his white eyes and retorted, "One day they'll ask. What will you tell them then?"

Star turned away, refusing to indulge his grumpy attitude. "I'll figure that out when I have to," she answered. "Besides, PapaMook will come soon and take us out of here."

"Right," Moon grumbled. "In the meantime, all we eat are seeds and nuts that the stickytoes bring. We never see the sky lights dance anymore. And PapaMook and Pesky are probably lost. I don't think there is a green forest in the south anyway. Barkbiters are everywhere! We shoulda' destroyed them when we could!" he finished, his face grim.

Star turned and spoke firmly to her younger brother. "We should be grateful to the stickytoes. The seeds and nuts they bring us are all they can find anymore. The magnificent dancing sky lights are there whether we see them or not. The green South Forest is there, too. The barkbiters have not reached it yet. And PapaMook and Pesky are probably already on their way back. Right now!" she added sharply.

Moon shrugged his shoulders. Suddenly, he spoke up, his voice hopeful. "Look, Star. Veil wants you!" He waved to the huge, swaying shadow of the looksalot.

Star glanced over her shoulder to look at Veil.

The looksalot slowly lifted his two-toed front hand and waved at her. His smoky green scales turned from green to gray as he blended into the cave wall behind him. His tail unwound as he balanced his oversized body to signal Star. His eyes rolled around, one aimed at Star and the other at Moon. Then his eyes rolled again, one aimed at the entrance and another at a bug caught in the shimmering spider web.

Star stepped quickly over to Veil and patted his nose affectionately. Unexpectedly, with amazing speed, he shot out his incredibly long, sticky tongue and snatched the bug struggling in the sticky web. He pulled it back into his flat mouth and crunched it slowly and thoughtfully. Star waited patiently.

Nearby a trickle of water ran down the granite wall and splashed into a shallow bowl of water. Star listened to the soft rush of the cold water as it spilled over the bowl and onto the earth, lost in a deep crack in the clay.

The legs of the huge bug stuck out from Veil's wide mouth and kicked frantically. Finally Veil gobbled the legs and swallowed them, too. The looksalot tossed his head at the webs. He rocked back and forth in slow motion a few times to indicate Star should look through the sticky mass.

Star brightened at once and gazed through the thick spider strands into the gray mist beyond. She saw nothing outside, but trusted that Veil felt vibrations in the earth. He always knew if something was approaching the cave long before she did. Suddenly, Star called over her shoulder. "The stickytoes are coming! Come help me!" She stepped to the web and lifted it up to allow a narrow passage for the stickytoes. Moon quickly stepped over to help lift the web.

A high-stepping procession of three muddy colored, orange-speckled stickytoes darted into the cave. Their eyes were moist and deep brown. They swept their tails constantly. Their mouths formed eternal mysterious smiles. Their toes were actually small, round pods that stuck to any surface they wished to climb. If the mood struck them, the stickytoes would scurry up the cave walls and across the ceiling just as if the stone surfaces were flat ground.

Now the three stickytoes pressed their bellies on the ground and nodded their heads. Moss bags—stuffed to nearly bursting—slipped from girdles on their backs and fell heavily beside them. Seeds, nuts, and grass spilled out.

The excited Twig babes leapt from their moss beds and rushed over. Star shooed the tiny, curious fingers away from the food. The stickytoes clicked their tongues sharply, chirped a few merry whistles, and grinned at Star, Moon, and Veil.

Star reached out gratefully to her devoted stickytoes, kissed each one between the eyes, and stroked their smooth, spotted heads. She grabbed some clumps of wet moss and dipped them in the shallow bowl of water. She squeezed the moss, and water dribbled slowly over the stickytoes' skin.

They grinned, then one at a time, licked their own eyes with a smooth, quick swipe of their long, pink tongues. Lovingly, they blinked at Star.

These bizarre creatures were her dearest and most loyal friends. Veil could rest for a while. Click, Chirp, and Crunch were back.

Star sighed with relief.

The night guards had arrived.

CHAPTER FOUR

LEAF AND PESKY

"Please . . . please give Pesky . . . food . . . ." Mook's voice trailed off. He was extremely weak and could hardly speak at all. The slurring words he mustered were full of concern for his tooler companion, Pesky. "Please . . . Pesky . . . food!" Mook's head fell back on Leaf's soft moss bed.

Mumma lifted his head up again, encouraging him to sip some warm mint tea. Fern placed cool moss packs on his head. Mook waved them both away, murmured some garbled words, moaned, and then turned on his side and sobbed.

Mumma urged Leaf, "Go on, Leaf. See that Pesky has food."

Leaf stood in the doorway of his sleeping hollow where Mook lay ill and restless on his moss bed. Now the young Twig stepped over and skeptically looked out the knothole to the limb beyond.

Pesky was nearby, never straying far from his dear friend Mook. He was hopping along a broad branch and poking his sharp, yellow beak into any crevice he could find. The tooler yanked out juicy worms and gulped them down as quickly as he could.

He doesn't appear to need any food, Leaf thought wryly. He stepped back to peek in his hollow.

Urgently, Mumma pressed two juicy, red huckleberries into Leaf's hands. "Here now, Leaf, please give these to Pesky." Then she turned to Mook and spoke loudly. "Leaf is feeding Pesky right now, Mook. Please don't worry. Now sip some of this lovely mint tea."

Mook ignored her entreaties and continued to mumble. "Pesky . . . give food . . . Pesky!"

Exasperated, Mumma immediately pushed Leaf toward the knothole. "Go on, Leaf. Feed that silly tooler," she said impatiently.

Reluctantly, Leaf stepped out of the knothole onto the broad branch beyond and stared at Pesky. Not picky at all, the tooler gobbled down every wriggly bug he found and pointedly ignored the hesitant, young Twig.

It was twilight. The sun's last pink streaks raced across the sky, shooting out over the immense Sharp Peaks that bordered Leaf's forest. Tree frogs chirped cheerfully in the dusky light as they clung to the rough bark. Now the evening shadows allowed them freedom. Ready to sleep, the birds tucked their heads under their wings in high, spreading branches. A light breeze ruffled Leaf's green, leafy hair. Pesky kept poking the tree bark.

Leaf stood back, unsure if the tooler was tame with strangers. Pesky was tall enough to easily knock him off the limb if he should startle the busy bird. Leaf stretched out his hand toward Pesky with one of the huckleberries in it. Pesky froze for an instant then tilted his head. In a blur of feathers, he snatched the berry from Leaf's fingers. Noticing Leaf held another behind his back, Pesky plucked the berry from Leaf's other hand, and nearly pushed him off the branch. Pesky rudely examined Leaf's hands and, seeing there were no more berries, turned away to search the furrows in the branch again.

Irritated, Leaf decided he had had enough of the tooler. He stepped back through the knothole into the haven and looked over his shoulder with annoyance. He muttered under his breath, "That stupid tooler couldn't possibly still be hungry. He acts like he's never had food!"

Mook cried out sharply from Leaf's hollow, "Star . . . Star . . . the babes! Pesky will take us." Then he moaned and mumbled many confusing words, as if in a trance.

Mumma pushed Buddy and Burba into their own hollow. "Stay there!" she ordered. Then she caught Pappo's eye and motioned to him to step away so Mook could not hear them speak.

Nosey as always, Fern pushed her way into the huddle. "What's that strange old Twig saying?" asked Fern plaintively. "It sounds like he's saying there are Twig babes alone somewhere and Pesky can find them!" Fern was obviously frustrated with Mook's flailing around and incoherent mutters. She stared dismally at Leaf's hollow, where Mook lay. "And what's a Star? Is that his home? Is a Star his haven?" she badgered Mumma and Pappo for answers they didn't have. "He's really weird, you know," Fern finished.

"Fern, remember your manners," Mumma said sternly. Then she added, "Fern, he doesn't know what he's saying. Babes would never be left alone, and you're right, Star is probably the name of his haven. Mook is very ill and he's probably just dream talking. He may not even know where he is or what he's saying at all." Mumma ended the conversation with Fern and dismissed her. "You belong with Buddy and Burba. Go on now."

Resigned to not understanding anything, Fern nodded. She threw the unused moss pack to the floor, glad to be free from helping an old Twig who didn't want to be helped. She stomped off.

With a very worried expression, Mumma turned to Pappo and lowered her voice to a soft whisper. "Pappo, Mook is very sick. I saw this once before, a long time ago when I was young. I'm sure he has brittlebark. He'll only get worse and worse if he doesn't get proper care."

"What can we do?" asked Pappo.

Leaf waited politely by the knothole and strained to hear their whispers which he could not make out. Pappo and Mumma's quiet murmurs floated like dust in the air. Abruptly, Leaf stepped over and stood between them. *He should be included*, he thought. Leaf stood silent.

Pappo glanced at his young son but did not send him away. "Is there a cure for it?"

Mumma rubbed her tired face. "The only cure I know for brittlebark is to pack him in ice for a day. I don't know how we can manage that, though, in this warm season."

Pappo spoke up at once. "There is always the great snow and ice pack on Echo Peak. We can pack him in the Long Ice. If there is a way to get him there, the Long Ice will save him." Pappo tilted his head and rubbed his chin as he pondered the possibility.

"Whisper can carry him!" Leaf interrupted.

Mumma and Pappo turned to stare at him. "She can?" they asked in disbelief.

"Yes," said Leaf. "If you can make a riding chair, Pappo, she'll carry him to Echo Peak."

Considering this idea for a moment, Pappo slapped his hands together and exclaimed, "Yes! That's a good idea, Leaf! Whisper is the gentlest chipmunk I've ever seen! Come help me tie a chair on her now. We've no time to lose."

Mumma laid a hand on Pappo's arm and said, worried, "You'll travel at night?"

Pappo placed his hands on her shoulders and spoke firmly. "Mook needs to be packed in ice as soon as possible, right? And we won't know why he came here or what is wrong in the North Forest until he can tell us. So, we have no choice. I must take him to the Long Ice now."

"I'll come too!" Leaf piped up eagerly.

With a stern look, Pappo answered, "You'll stay here and help Mumma!"

"But . . ." Leaf frowned as his words died away. He knew better than to argue.

Without another word, Pappo sprang swiftly through the haven's knothole, dropped through the Old Seeder's branches, and plopped onto a large spongy mushroom. Leaf swung down through the tree limbs and landed clumsily on some damp moss.

"Whisper, come to me, Whisper!" Leaf called out low.

A freckled, furry face with stiff whiskers, tufted ears, and warm brown eyes peeked out of a knothole, not far above Leaf's head. Whisper yawned and scratched her ear with tiny claws. She had just gone to sleep for the night, but she scampered from her warm bed anyway. She circled Leaf a few times, then squatted happily beside him and wrapped her striped tail around them both. Leaf stood only a little taller than Whisper. Her quivering whiskers tickled his nose. She sniffed his leafy head and nibbled on his green leafy hair.

"Stop now, Whisper, stop," Leaf laughed. "Hey, you silly chipmunk, we need your help tonight. Can you help us out?"

Whisper tilted her head, batted her long-lashed, brown eyes, and stared seriously at Leaf.

"I need you to carry an old, sick Twig to the Long Ice with Pappo tonight," said Leaf. "Can you do that for me?"

Whisper listened carefully. She did not understand Leaf's words, but she always understood his meaning. She nodded. Anything for her Leaf! Their bond was exceptionally strong. Not so long ago, Whisper had carried Leaf all the way across the wide valley, through many dangers, and brought him safely to his haven here in the Old Seeder. To be near her dear Leaf, she had remained and made this place her home too.

Now Whisper twitched her whiskers quickly to indicate her enthusiasm for the new mission she was given. She groomed her fluffy tail at once to prepare herself for the journey.

Pappo fashioned a carrying cradle from his long, flaxen rope. He tested its strength by tugging on the knots then he and Leaf placed it on Whisper's back, just behind her freckled, furry shoulders. Pappo wrapped the rope twice around her chest and under her white, fuzzy belly. It was secure.

At last, Pappo turned to Leaf and placed his hand on his shoulder. "Leaf," he said, "you must distract Pesky. Tie him to a limb and feed him berries. Mook and I must be invisible in the forest at night. Pesky will only hurt himself if he tries to follow us. He'll bring too much attention to us from night stalkers like owls and foxes."

"Yes, Pappo," Leaf nodded. He understood completely.

"Go now," Pappo directed him and pointed up to where Pesky still hopped around in the branches. "I'll bring Mook down on my back when Pesky isn't looking."

Leaf climbed quickly up the massive trunk of the Old Seeder. He dove into the haven's knothole and scooped up handfuls of huckleberries, seeds, and mashcakes. He stuffed them in a moss bag and stepped out of the knothole. Pappo was waiting there. Leaf nodded to him— the trick was underway. Leaf climbed up the trunk and crawled out onto a branch just above the tooler.

"Pesky. Look, Pesky. Look here," chirped Leaf. He waved a berry around in the dark.

Pesky looked up and then back at the haven's knothole. Pappo disappeared inside. Mook's moans hung in

the air. Pesky looked up again, eyeing the berry greedily. He hopped up on a higher branch, then another,
and another. He stepped carefully along the limb and
perched near Leaf. With a flurry of feathers, he plucked
the berry from Leaf's hand. Before he could turn to hop
back down, Leaf held out another. This time he held
it behind his back so Pesky had to stretch his neck out
to get it. When Pesky stabbed at the berry, his braided
leash fell easily into Leaf's other hand. Quickly, Leaf
tied it to a knobby limb nearby.

Pesky looked down at the braid and noticed he was
now tied up, but it didn't seem to bother him much. Leaf
wondered if he was usually tied up someplace. *The silly
tooler is probably completely tame*, he thought. He felt
smug because he had caught Pesky so easily. Casually,
Leaf tossed him another berry. The tooler snatched it
out of the air even though it was now very dark.

Below, Pappo crawled from the knothole with Mook
slung across his back. He quickly slipped down through
the limbs to Whisper, who munched on clover tips and
waited patiently. Leaf held up a berry to distract Pesky
again, but the tooler spotted Pappo and Mook and
became anxious. He tugged hard at his leash. Leaf held
the braid firmly and drew him back.

Leaf tried to soothe the confused tooler. "I'm sorry, Pesky, but you can't go with Mook," Leaf told him. "Don't worry. Pappo's taking him to the Long Ice, so he can get well. Don't worry." Leaf sat beside Pesky and held his braid until the tooler stopped tugging.

Finally Pesky grew still. He stared at Leaf. His eyes were black and intense as if he were deciding whether or not Leaf could be trusted. Leaf held up another berry. Pesky took it at once and chirped. Evidently he decided Leaf must not be all bad. The tooler searched the limb between his claws for more worms then with a quick flurry of dust, Pesky puffed up to twice his size, pulled each feather through his beak, and groomed himself to perfection.

Leaf smiled. Pesky would be all right. Leaf looked down through the drooping branches. Two fleeting shadows raced up a forest trail that led to Echo Peak. Leaf knew it would take all night and a day for Pappo, Mook, and Whisper to reach the Long Ice. Hopefully, the ice pack would cure Mook of brittle-bark and they would understand why the sick, old Twig had flown all this way. *But what if Mook didn't recover? Would Pappo travel to the North Forest anyway?*

Leaf stared at Echo Peak. The white-capped mountain loomed above him, silent and forbidding in the dark sky. It was so immense it blocked most of the evening stars. Leaf turned and stared at the faraway north sky over the Sharp Peaks.

What was there?

CHAPTER FIVE

LEAF FLIES NORTH

Leaf suddenly felt restless, and he didn't want to go to sleep yet. He watched an enormous owl soar from its perch and hunt in the dark sky. Pesky hopped over and pecked Leaf's head with his beak. It hurt.

"Hey," Leaf exclaimed. "I don't have any worms on my head! Go dig some up somewhere else!" Then, unexpectedly, a surprising idea came to him. A tooler probably knew how to find his way better than a Twig. Why couldn't Pesky find Mook's haven by himself? Leaf rubbed his chin, thinking. Were Twig babes really left up there all alone? Could Pesky even find them by himself? Leaf realized that if someone in the North Forest really did need help, maybe *he* could rescue them *before* Pappo returned.

Finally, Leaf slapped his knee. He had decided. He would fly north on Pesky at dawn. He was sure he'd be back before Pappo. Leaf felt happy at once. He kissed Pesky on his beak. Surprised, Pesky paused from digging in the bark for a moment. Excited, Leaf looked north at the dark sky above the Sharp Peaks. But for a moment he hesitated, unsure. It seemed so far away. Were there really dancing lights in the sky? He wondered what else might be there.

The soft rustling of the Old Seeder's fronds hushed the birds to sleep, yet Pesky still stuffed himself with night worms. Usually birds perched and slept at night, but not this tooler. Leaf knew they both must rest, but his thoughts were racing now. He wondered if Pesky would let him climb on his back. What if Pesky didn't know the way and they were lost? Mook said Pesky could find his home, but Mook was very sick. Was it just dream talking? *In any case, someone has to see if Twig babes really are left alone in the North Forest,* Leaf reassured himself. *It might as well be me.* He looked at the wavering stars floating sleepily in the north sky. Somewhere over there lay the Land of Dancing Sky

Lights, whatever that meant. Somewhere beyond those high, jagged mountains was, what?

Leaf crept quietly to the gash below the haven's knot-hole. Silently he pulled out Mumma's hunting tools - her rope, strap, saver, and her precious whistletube. He climbed back up to sit by Pesky, who still scraped the bark for treats. He opened his moss bag and took out all of the seeds, berries, and mashcakes. Then he stuffed them in the pockets of the shoulder strap. *These eats should do for a little while,* thought Leaf. There's sure to be more in the North Forest, if needed. Besides, Pesky didn't need more treats! His belly looked like it would burst!

"You must rest," Leaf whispered to the tooler. "You need to take me to the Land of Dancing Sky Lights in the morning. We will fly to Star, Mook's haven. You must sleep now."

At the sound of Leaf's words, Pesky tilted his head to one side as if he recognized the names Leaf spoke. His eyes gleamed in the dark like sparkling black stones.

Startled at Pesky's strange, unblinking gaze, Leaf stared back and asked tentatively, "Pesky, do you know how to get back to the Land of Dancing Sky Lights?"

Pesky stepped briskly up to Leaf and bowed his head. He seemed to be offering a ride at that very moment. Surprised, Leaf stood up and reached out to stroke the tooler's green and indigo feathers. He murmured, "In the morning, my friend. We'll go at dawn."

Pesky turned his back to Leaf and waited patiently for him to climb on as if expecting to fly away at once.

Leaf stroked Pesky's neck some more. "Maybe you're not so stupid after all, Pesky," Leaf said. Then he realized the tooler would probably not rest at all now. Leaf pulled out the whistletube and blew a lovely, slow melody. The soothing song curled gently among the fronds of the Old Seeder and melted away into the shadows. The birds stirred, fluffed up their feathers, and then tucked their heads back under their wings. Soon Pesky's head drooped too. He gripped the limb tightly with his thin, sharp claws, and tucked his head beneath his wing. Finally, he fell asleep. Leaf crept silently away to lie down in his hollow.

At daybreak, rosy streaks stretched above the Sharp Peaks. Leaf woke up as the last chirps of the night frogs were ending. Soon early morning birds and blue blossoms would lift their heads together and greet the sweet-scented day. Leaf sat up immediately. He tiptoed from his hollow.

Near the haven's doorway, Mumma knelt and poured water into a cappynut shell. Her braided rope lay curled up neatly and her whistletube hung from a thorn hook on the shoulder strap. The strap was lumpy with food stuffed in the pockets. The walking stick, her saver, was usually tucked into the strap's back loop but instead the sturdy stick leaned against the wall. The pale blue stone wedged into the knothole at the tip of the saver caught the morning rays and threw a shimmering rainbow across the wall.

"Mumma," Leaf whispered urgently, "you can't go to the North Forest. You are not well enough to travel. You're not yet mended from your terrible fall last season. I must go. I must take Pesky to find Mook's haven. If there are babes there, I will help them, not you." He waited, worried by her silent preparations for travel.

She stepped over to Leaf, and her willowy fingers brushed out his emerald green leaves, tangled up from the night's sleep. She lifted her bulging strap over his head and across one shoulder. Quickly, she wrapped her rope around his waist and over his other shoulder then tucked her saver through the strap's back loop.

She tugged on the whistletube's string to be sure it was secure. Satisfied at last, she shook his shoulders gently and said, "Of course you must go, Leaf. I've been worried too. Perhaps there are babes up north alone and maybe they need help. I wish I could travel, but you're right. I'm not well enough." She paused and then said seriously, "Return home swiftly! You know Pappo will go searching for you if you are not here when he comes back."

"Don't worry, Mumma," Leaf answered, grateful for her encouragement. "I'll return right away." He hooked the cappynut shell full of cool water on his strap then jumped through the knothole and into the cool mist of dawn. "Bye, Mumma," he whispered.

Leaf heard her soft voice floating after him. "Good luck, dear Leaf!"

Leaf was surprised to see Pesky awake. The tooler was brutally attacking the old tree's worms once more. Leaf approached Pesky, reached out one hand, and laid it on his beak. With his other hand, he caught the tooler's golden, braided leash.

Leaf addressed the tooler firmly. "Pesky, you and I are flying to the Land of Dancing Sky Lights now. We will find Mook's haven, Star!" Pesky nodded his head vigorously, ruffled his feathers from the tip of his stubby tail to top of his head, and flapped his wings three times to tell Leaf he was ready to go. Leaf smiled broadly. He leapt on Pesky's back and buried his skinny stick legs deep under the soft feathers on Pesky's wings. All set, he cried out, "Let's go!"

Pesky skipped a few sideways hops down the length of the branch. When he reached the end, he sprang at once into the cool dawn air. His strong wings lifted him up and up, higher and higher!

Leaf held the braid so tight his fingers hurt. They rushed into the startling blue sky until they soared breathlessly above the Old Seeder itself! Pesky flew in a circle above the ancient tree a few times as if checking to find the right direction. Then he spiraled away and flew off toward the jagged Sharp Peaks. The dawn spread like crimson water flowing over the peaks but Leaf only felt its burning rays on his arms. He clung to Pesky's back and buried his woody face in Pesky's wind-ruffled feathers, afraid to look.

After a long while of smooth flying, Leaf mustered his courage and peeked over Pesky's shoulders. Pesky's wings stretched out wide and steady beside him. The two floated aloft, nearly motionless. Pesky barely beat his wings. The sky was bright blue. Far below, a rolling fog drifted stubbornly above crooked, wandering rivers. The tooler tucked his legs up tightly under his belly. It increased his speed. Blurry trees raced by beneath them and Leaf felt dizzy. The wind sliced like ice through his leafy hair.

Leaf clung so desperately to Pesky's braid that it took him awhile to unclench his fists—one knotty finger at a time. Leaf gulped the icy air. Suddenly, and unexpectedly, he felt thrilled from his green, leafy head to his dark, curly toes! Being so high felt glorious! Flying so fast—incredible! He was really flying on a tooler!

Pesky twitched his wings and caught another swiftly-flowing stream of air. Leaf noticed the tooler was oddly alert and watched the skies warily as they flew. With a shiver Leaf realized Pesky was searching for danger. *He must be worried about eagles and falcons. We're not safe. Even this fast. Even this high.* Leaf gripped the braid tighter and carefully sat straighter. Far ahead lay a smoky, brown horizon. *Where are all the green trees?* Leaf wondered. *Why is it so brown in the North Forest? It isn't smoke. Could the North Forest be filled with brown trees? That's not possible.* Leaf laughed. *How silly.* He wondered what it could be.

Before long, Pesky spiraled down in a wide circle, lower and lower. Leaf noticed that he flew toward a pool of still water. The pond was surrounded by a pretty meadow and lay peacefully in the middle of sloping foothills. *Pesky must need to eat and rest,* Leaf realized. *Good idea!*

Pesky skidded clumsily to a stop at the pond's edge. He dug his claws into the mud to keep from sliding into the water. Abruptly Pesky shook Leaf from his back and tossed him into a patch of sweet-smelling, pink daisies. Their blossoms clung to Leaf's head but he was grateful to feel the earth again. His legs were wobbly. His hands shook as he pulled seeds from his strap and offered some to Pesky. The tooler simply seized a plump caterpillar wriggling on a daisy petal. Leaf noticed there were many fat bugs squirming around in the mud on the bank of the pond. He wondered if Pesky spotted them as he flew over the water. He chuckled at the thought. *It's a wonder he ever gets anywhere if he can see bugs from so high up.*

Leaf sat cross-legged among the daisies and munched happily on a few seeds. Thirsty from the scary flight, he drank all the water from his cappynut, so he walked over to refill the shell from the pond. As he stood knee deep in the water, he glanced around the meadow. White butterflies floated from blossom to blossom and fluttered erratically in the breeze. Tiny green and yellow birds sang short, cheerful melodies to each other. They seemed to be discussing where would be the best places to find bugs and seeds.

The sun was hot. Leaf sprinkled some water on his head. After his cappynut was refilled, he hooked it on his strap and then looked around. Shadows wavered beneath the willowy trees lining the edge of the small meadow. White, fluffy wisps of dandelions tore from the stems' tips and floated with the breeze across the pond. Long grass trembled in the water as silver minnows sucked at their roots. It looked so peaceful.

But something felt odd. Leaf caught his breath. Pesky was nowhere in sight! He stifled a cry and instinctively crouched as he looked up at the sky. What had happened? Did an eagle snatch him up? Or did Pesky simply fly away and abandon him? Leaf moved quickly to check every shadow, every bush, and every patch of grass in the meadow.

Pesky was gone!

CHAPTER SIX

THE LAND OF DANCING SKY LIGHTS

"Moon, come sit beside me." Star spoke kindly, yet firmly, to her younger brother. She knew he tried to hide his feelings by being rude and grumpy, but Star refused to indulge his bitterness. Moon tossed his white, leafy hair and blinked his colorless eyes at Star. He shrugged his shoulders stubbornly, turned away, and leaned on the cold stone wall. He did not need company.

"No," he replied gruffly.

"Moon," Star insisted patiently, "how about a story? It will help to pass the time." She looked up hopefully.

The babes happily played with sparkling stones across the cave from where she sat cross-legged. She continued to keep an eye on them; although, they were intent on their game of rolling and smashing stones in a shallow, winding rut they had scratched in the clay.

Moon shrugged again, then turned halfway to mutter, "How about the story of PapaMook and the spirit bears?" he asked.

"Sure!" Star responded brightly. "Now come on and sit here with me!"

Moon reluctantly plopped down near Star and rested his elbows on his knees. His long, skinny fingers tugged at his leafy, white hair. He stared at the ground and studied his toes.

"All right," said Star. "The story of the spirit bears!" She settled comfortably into a hollow on the cave floor. Her voice was low and soft in the cave. She began as she always did.

Star explained how Twigs wandered at some time or another. They set off on adventures to test their Twig skills and hunting tools. They wandered to learn about the world they lived in. Dangers were familiar, and PapaMook was unafraid. But that was a time when the North Forest was green.

PapaMook was young when he set off to find the end of the West Forest and the mysterious spirit bear who lived there and slept in the trunks of giant cedar trees. He had heard unbelievable old stories. Supposedly, the furthermost edge of the west land was smothered in water which looked like a murky sky. He had heard that a white bear with golden tipped fur appeared in icy creeks, caught enormous fish then disappeared into the lush forest as if it were invisible.

Star told how PapaMook wandered to a rain-drenched place far west, tangled with enormous trees like none he'd seen before. Their limbs hung heavy, wet with shimmering drops of water which sparkled so brilliantly they glistened like ice. And hungry wolves howled all the time.

PapaMook went into the strange world prepared for danger. He had his hunting tools, of course, but he also brought a silver leaf from a poplar tree to hide beneath. He wore the leaf tied over his head. Not only did it help him blend into the damp, trampled paths, it helped keep his leafy hair dry, too. But the leaf was not enough to keep from being constantly drenched by the continuous, cold rain. Still, PapaMook was determined to find the dark water which supposedly pressed against the West

Forest. He especially hoped to catch sight of the white spirit bear.

PapaMook struggled on faint trails beneath soggy, dripping branches for days until suddenly the land plunged from a cliff into a vast, deathly still, watery reflection of a stormy sky. Far away across the deep, flat water, lone islands floated through a swirling, thick mist. The scattered, isolated land appeared to drift about in the fog. Disturbing cries of the howling wolves echoed across the quiet water and PapaMook shuddered. He turned away from the ghostly warning. He wished to see no more of the gloomy West Forest. He didn't even want to search for the spirit bears anymore. He only wanted to go home.

PapaMook retreated hastily into the silent, rain-burdened trees. He rushed to return home to the North Forest but the trails became twisted and unfamiliar. He tried this path, then that path, then another path but soon he knew he was lost. The random tracks of creatures and their scattered paw marks only led him back to his own confused steps. PapaMook wandered for days, weary, and soaked. The continual drip of rain depressed him even more. He grew more worried and afraid for he could find no path from the West Forest.

Finally, after a long while, PapaMook threw himself onto a mound of frosty leaves and lay there in despair. The sun briefly burst through the fog but even this unexpected shaft of sunlight did nothing to cheer him. But he was not alone.

Suddenly, the latticed leaves beneath him tore apart and he nearly fell into a dark knothole! An old cedar tree lay sideways, decaying on the forest floor, buried under huge clumps of moss and overgrown ferns. PapaMook grasped hold of the wet bark and clung on desperately. At once, he felt an odd sensation of warmth. Puffballs of misty breath drifted up from deep within the enormous hollow trunk. Some beast—more than one—breathed and snored in an eerie, calm, rhythmic murmur. PapaMook froze, balanced awkwardly over the crumbling knothole, terrified he'd wake the slumbering beasts which had stuffed themselves into this massive, cedar log.

Suddenly he heard a great snorting and *crunch, crunch, crunch* rushing up swiftly behind him. Horrified, PapaMook lost his hold and fell straight down through the knothole. He plunged into the beasts' hidden den and landed on thick, fuzzy fur. He heard soft snores and smelled milk on the muzzles of three fluffy spirit bear cubs—two black cubs and one white.

At once, a large shadow blocked the sunlight streaming down through the knothole. A heavy, snorting, sucking, slobbering panting took its place. A huge black nose pushed into the knothole but the opening was too small for the beast's great head. The beast angrily circled the log, searching for a way into the den.

The cubs woke, startled by the frenzied scratching and grunting outside their warm haven. Terrified, they whimpered and tried to bury themselves in the scattered leaves and moss covering the floor of their den.

Outside, the beast shoved the cedar log but the ancient trunk refused to roll. Frustrated the beast beat the mighty trunk but it would not break. A furious growl erupted, and the horrible noise panicked the cubs. They began a wailing, pitiful cry for help, and frantically crawled over one another to reach the furthest end of the log.

PapaMook dove from one clump of leaves to another to keep from being trampled to death.

Finally, the beast squeezed through the matted roots of the hollow trunk. With a burst of smelly, hot breath its great head appeared in the den but the roots were too thick and tangled. They held the beast back from the cubs. The beast ripped out pieces of its own bristling, muddy-looking fur as it struggled against the roots to reach the cubs.

Even as PapaMook cringed, horrified and afraid, he recognized the long, brutal teeth and ugly muzzle of a lone, male, shadow bear. If the shadow bear had such a terrible hunger that it hunted bear cubs, the spirit bear cubs had no chance against it!

With a ravenous snarl, the bear slammed against the thick jumble of roots! A huge paw reached through and clawed the air wildly inside the den. It pushed its huge black nose in as far as it could, and sucked in the air greedily to find the sweet scent of the cubs. Terrified, the poor cubs cried desperately for their mum. Instinctively they cowered and dodged the cruel claws of the shadow bear. They scrambled over each other to find some place safe from its horrible, drooling mouth and dagger-like teeth. But the den offered no corner in which to hide. With each tug against the roots, the beast's teeth snapped at them closer and closer!

PapaMook knew he must save the cubs, but what could he do? The starving bear was desperate and gigantic. PapaMook never felt so small! In their panic, the cubs had nearly crushed him flat. He had to act quickly, so he yanked his walking stick, his sturdy saver, out of its loop on his back, and swung it hard at the shadow bear's flailing claws. But it was easily slapped away. The saver whirled in the air and then stuck in the moss between his feet.

It was then that PapaMook knew just what he must do. Feeling oddly calm, PapaMook stepped quickly into the sunrays which flickered down from the knothole above his head. He stuck his saver deep into the crushed leaves and rolled it between his hands. A single sunbeam struck the stone which was stuck into the knothole at the top of the stick. The ray flashed brightly around the den, then shot out and burned into the wood of the trunk. PapaMook quickly aimed the brilliant beam right into the shadow bear's eyes.

The horrible beast shrieked! Twisting away from the stabbing light, it fought its way back out of the roots and, whimpering from the blazing-hot pain, fled into the forest.

But now the poor cubs cried even louder and cowered together in a fat ball of shivering, white fur. They did not understand they were safe. PapaMook grabbed his whistletube and sang a soothing melody to quiet their sobs. The cubs soon stopped sniffling, curled up around him, and nuzzled his hair, curious about this kind stick creature in their midst. After a long while, evening crept into their warm den and the marvelous, wavy colors of the northern night's sky lights flitted about high above the knothole. The saver lay on the den's floor and PapaMook noticed that its stone reflected the colors of the dancing sky. He picked up the walking stick and twisted it. The stone threw dazzling hues all over the cubs and the den. The tiny cubs sniffed the flickering lights and batted them playfully with their pink paws.

PapaMook did not notice the enormous, white spirit bear standing at the entrance to the den watching the lights and her cubs. Her expression was worried and puzzled. The cubs' mum had silently crept up, frightened at seeing the roots ripped from the hollow cedar den. She had smelled the horrific stench of the male shadow bear. She feared the worst. Now she blinked in surprise at her cubs' joyful play, enraptured by the reflected sky lights. She could not believe they were safe. Then she noticed her cubs had encircled a stick creature no taller than a blue jay. It was this odd creature who was flashing the pretty lights around the den with a stone stuck in a stick.

PapaMook glanced at the movement in the den's roots and froze. He stared at the giant, white head and huge, black nose of the spirit bear mum. Noticing the Twig's rigid posture, the sweet cubs sniffed him and pushed him over with their soft muzzles. Then they noticed their mum. Squealing with delight, they climbed on top of one another to reach her.

The spirit bear mum was thin from the cold season's fasting and slipped easily through the roots. She wriggled into their midst and licked their fuzzy faces to comfort them. By their high-pitched whines and trembling bodies, she was told that something terrible had happened. She knew their lives had been threatened by a foul, grisly beast. The strange whistling flute-song made by the stick creature had echoed in the forest, and brought her back to the den. *But how were her cubs saved?* Staring at the tiny Twig, she slowly came to the conclusion that this stick creature had somehow rescued her cubs. Perhaps it was the stone's lights or the whistling song. Perhaps the stick creature had a mysterious power. Whatever had saved them, the mum felt deeply grateful. *Her cubs were alive!* And even more bizarre, the spirit bear mum knew the cubs adored the stick creature. She decided the odd creature could remain in the den.

PapaMook sensed her acceptance. He reached out a trembling hand and she allowed him to caress a gigantic, curved, black claw. He breathed deeply, sat down, and played another whistletube melody for the cubs and the loving mum. After he finished his song, he twisted the saver's stone and flashed the amazing sky lights' colors around in the den until the cubs were lulled into sleep and lay peacefully snoring.

The next morning, PapaMook crawled out through the knotted roots and stood atop the great, moss-covered cedar log. Even though the sky was clear and blue, fat drops of rain plopped steadily on his head. Annoyed, he looked up and stared in wonder at a huge sparkling spider web stretching from one limb to the next, hanging just above him. It glittered with dazzling raindrops.

A creepy, speckled spider bounced in the middle of her gigantic, complex web. She was terribly irritated because the rain had made her invisible web visible. Painstakingly, she crept from one strand to another, seized each glittering drop of rain, and furiously flung it from her web right down onto PapaMook's head.

It was at that moment PapaMook realized the West Forest held a mysterious beauty all its own. The heavy, water-laden tree limbs dripped with a rhythmic melody, and high on its rocky cliffs silvery waterfalls appeared which had not been there the day before. Yet, the tangled West Forest was still an unfamiliar and lonely place to PapaMook. He was lost.

The forlorn Twig felt tremors in the log as the giant spirit bear stirred within, grunted, and rolled over. He looked down through the knothole and saw the mum nudge her cubs. They were very young, but now they must go hunting with her. She would not leave them alone again. She pushed them out through the cedar roots with her broad snout. They tumbled end over end, sliding around in the wet leaves. They loved the startling, fresh air and the dazzling, bright blue, morning sky.

The spirit bear mum sauntered casually off under the drooping tree limbs and glanced back to be sure all three cubs followed her. For the first time, PapaMook noticed that her white fur twinkled in the sunlight with mystifying, golden tips. A surprising splash of gold sprinkled the coat of the one white cub, too. Unaware of any danger, the cubs celebrated their new freedom. They rolled over and over then chased each other until they plowed clumsily into the rump of their mum. She shook her mighty head and grunted. Dashing off again, the cubs paused only long enough to smack sparkling splashes of water crystals at one another with their smooth, pink paws. They slid on the wet stones, bumped into each other, joyfully somersaulted across thick moss, and disappeared into a clump of soggy ferns. At once, they burst out from the ferns and playfully attacked one another.

The mum grunted impatiently at them as she continued along a well-trodden path. PapaMook watched them scamper along awkwardly after their mum. He was happy the sweet cubs were safe.

Suddenly, as if forgetting something, the spirit bear mum turned to look at the Twig who stood watching her and her cubs from atop the cedar log. She grunted once more, and blew out puffy mist clouds into the cool air. She shook her head so hard that her whole body shuddered—right down to her stumpy tail. She waved her massive head at PapaMook, almost as if she were telling him "Follow me!"

Surprised at her insistence, he decided he would. Perhaps she thought he was a pet or a doll for her cubs to play with. But whatever she thought, PapaMook knew he had nowhere else to go, so he might as well follow her and the cubs. They wandered around the West Forest for most of the day. PapaMook and the spirit bears wove in and out of ghostly looking trees, up a steep bluff, down another, and over another high ridge, on a path which made sense only to the spirit bear mum. Resigned to living now in the West Forest for a long, long time, PapaMook trailed along behind the cubs and enjoyed their silly play.

After a long trek, the mum stopped by a swift-flowing creek, and glanced over her shoulder at PapaMook as if to invite him to stand beside her. As he stepped closer, he knew at once where he was. Incredibly, they now stood at the edge of the West Forest. Across a grassy, flat meadow sprinkled with tiny, blue flowers grew the pale green, slender pine trees of the North Forest. The spirit bear mum had been leading him home! Somehow she must have known he needed a guide. Happy at the sight of his own tall, thin trees, PapaMook rushed to her and threw his skinny, brown arms around her muzzle. Because she was so large, it was all that he could embrace. He kissed her nose and she sneezed. A huge blast of hot air blew him over backwards.

PapaMook regained his balance, bowed formally to the gigantic bear, and then said gratefully, "I will always remember your kindness. I wish you and your beautiful cubs a good life!" Then he sprinted happily across the clearing to the North Forest.

PapaMook paused at the edge of his forest home and turned to search for his new spirit bear friends in the strange world of mighty, tangled trees and glimmering rain. Like a startling, mystical cloud, the spirit bear mum's ghostly form appeared at the edge of the meadow. Behind her trudged the white cub. Just then, the two black cubs popped out from the dark shadows of a hemlock tree and joined the march through the tall grass.

The spirit bear mum lumbered along the border of the West Forest. She reached a small hilltop and then, as if sensing the Twig were watching her, she turned and stared directly at PapaMook. She rose and stood up on her back legs. Her white fur glowed with a halo of gold, and her tremendous body was silhouetted against the bright blue sky. She waved her massive heavy paws at PapaMook, who stood at the edge of the pale, green forest.

PapaMook waved back with all his strength and jumped up and down. He hoped she saw him there against the tree trunks.

All three cubs joined her in her salute to their new friend. They rose up on their back legs too. The blue sky outlined their fuzzy, pudgy bodies. The cubs stood on their stubby legs and waved their paws around in circles. Then the mum dropped down, shook her heavy head at her cubs, turned, and disappeared over the hill.

PapaMook never saw her or her cubs again.

Star sat silent, waiting for her moody brother to say something. "Well?" she finally asked.

"Yes," said Moon with a sigh, "it's just the way mums told it."

"Good!" said Star emphatically and sharply nodded her head. "Then we'll never forget it."

CHAPTER SEVEN

MOOK
AND THE LONG ICE

Whisper carried Mook—still weak and sick—uphill, through a steep pass in the blue Sharp Peaks toward Echo Peak. Pappo led the way. They had climbed to a place where few trees lived. Only stiff, sharp needles sprouted on the ancient, twisted trunks which suffered in the witheringly freezing wind. The icy air was difficult to breathe, yet the sweet, speckled chipmunk carried Mook gently and stepped gingerly among the loose rocks. They traveled all night and now, in the late morning sun, they finally stopped to rest in the shade of a rocky overhang.

Pappo lifted the frail, old Twig from the cradle on Whisper's back and laid him on the sand beside a massive boulder. Mook was restless. He mumbled panicked, garbled words Pappo could not understand. Pappo poured cool water in a stone hollow for Whisper and in the cap of his cappynut shell for Mook. He lifted the shell to Mook's lips but, again, the fragile Twig waved it away, still insisting they should care for Pesky first.

Pappo was greatly concerned about his weak patient. "You must drink, Mook. Don't worry about Pesky. He has food. Pesky is with Leaf. You must drink and eat," he insisted. Pappo sprinkled some water on Mook's face. "Please, Mook, please!"

Mook suddenly waved his arms about and shouted, "Watch out! Watch out! The biters! They're crawling! They're crawling! They're on the move!" He struggled to rise, then tumbled back and fell into a deep stupor.

Pappo looked around, expecting to see horrible bugs creeping toward them over the gravel, but he saw nothing. He looked at Whisper, a question in his eyes, to see if the chipmunk saw something. She did not. Whisper just shook her head and delicately scratched her tufted ear with the dainty claws on her back foot.

Pappo shrugged and muttered, "He must be dream talking again. Come on, Whisper. The sooner we can pack him in ice, the sooner he'll get well." Pappo lifted the still unconscious Twig gently into the cradle on Whisper's back and tied him in securely. Then he took the braided lead around Whisper's neck and walked up the steep, rocky trail. He looked ahead and studied the mountain pass. Pappo had not been on Echo Peak for a very long time, but he knew the Long Ice lay just beyond the top of the trail crest.

After a tiring walk nearly straight uphill, Pappo reached the crest. "There, Whisper! Look!" he said excitedly. "Just beyond those rocks is the Long Ice. I haven't been here for many seasons, but I remember the gulch ends here and the Long Ice sits right over that ridge!" Now Pappo quickened his step. Whisper followed close behind as the Twig carefully found footing on the loose gravel. Finally, Pappo stood on top of the jagged ridge. He looked around, bewildered.

The Long Ice wasn't there! Pappo anxiously tugged Whisper's leash to bring her up beside him.

"Whisper, something terrible has happened! The Long Ice has disappeared!" Pappo scanned the hillside back and forth, confused. "This makes no sense,

Whisper! The Long Ice is eternal. But it's not here! Am I lost?"

Whisper did not understand why her friend was so distressed, so she trembled with fear. Something was very wrong, but she didn't know what. She covered her face with her fuzzy paws.

Then Pappo caught a glimmer of white sparkles much further up the mountainside. He realized that the Long Ice had moved, or maybe melted, and now lay high up on the pinnacle of Echo Peak. How very strange. But at least, the ice was still here. *Perhaps it is not eternal after all,* thought Pappo. *It must be shrinking because of the too hot seasons.*

In any case, Pappo was greatly relieved to see it. He hung his arm around Whisper's neck to steady his shaky legs. "Oh, Whisper. It will be all right." He tried to soothe the frightened chipmunk. He pointed high up the hill. "There. There it is. For some reason, it is melting and fading away." Pappo shook his head, troubled. But to reassure Whisper, he added, "It's all right, though. Don't worry, Whisper. We can take Mook up that far."

At the sound of his name, Mook woke up. He struggled against the ropes holding him in his cradle. He was very confused again. He kicked his legs hard, trying to free himself. His feet dug into Whisper's side. His fists boxed her ears. Annoyed, Whisper bucked. Mook grabbed Whisper's furry hair and glared wildly at nothing. Then, all at once, a scream erupted from the old Twig and he shrieked, "They're coming! They're coming! The biters! Run! Run! Star! Moon! Grab the babes! Run to the cave! Run!"

Pappo was shocked. He simply stared at Mook kicking Whisper and pulling her hair out.

But Whisper had had enough of Mook's crazy ranting. Even if this frail, old Twig *was* sick, she wasn't going to carry him any further. She shook her shoulders vigorously. Mook and his rope cradle spilled onto a pile of rocks. Whisper hopped briskly away, satisfied to be rid of the weird, screaming, old Twig at last. She climbed on a flat rock and licked her bare patches.

Pappo suddenly shouted, "Whisper, look out!"

Whisper looked at him, irritated. *Now what,* she seemed to ask. Then she saw the shadow. It was moving swiftly—like water running over rocks—directly at her. Whisper dove from her flat rock into a shallow rut. But there was no cover there! She heard a horrific *screech!* An eagle hunted her! Her paws slid out from under her on loose gravel. She scrambled to find safety and streaked back and forth across the steep ridge, desperately seeking a hole or crevice in which to hide. But the hillside was barren and the eagle's shadow followed her closely across the rocks as quickly as she could run.

Behind a large boulder on top of the ridge, far above Whisper's frantic scrambling, a cruel beast crouched. It was even hungrier than the eagle and now it licked its whiskers and watched the panicked chipmunk stumble in the loose rocks. Its hair bristled on its back and it crouched, ready to leap down the hill. Its gray tail switched nervously. Its yellow, pitiless eyes narrowed. The angry wolf had been stalking the chipmunk from the moment he saw her on the ridge. Now it was furious that the eagle attacked the chipmunk and it dared to snatch away its morning meal! No more skulking behind boulders now! The wolf had no fear of an eagle, so immediately it launched itself straight downhill in pursuit of the chipmunk!

Whisper crisscrossed the ridge wildly, desperate to find shelter. She climbed further uphill with each pass. Luckily she outmaneuvered the eagle and its sharp claws at each turn but still, there was no crevice or crack, no place to hide!

Now the wolf and the eagle both pursued Whisper! One flew above, and the other raced madly down the mountain. She was trapped!

All the while, Mook kept shrieking, "Watch out! The biters! The biters!"

Pappo raced uphill after Whisper and hastily drew out his saver from its loop. But he could not get solid footing on the loose gravel. No matter how desperately he tried, he could not get close enough to the eagle to battle its outstretched claws. Just as he slipped again, Pappo looked uphill. Shocked, he saw the wolf streaking downhill straight at Whisper!

Horrified, he screamed, "Hide, Whisper! A wolf hunts you! Hide!"

If Whisper heard the screams of Pappo, she gave no sign because just then she spotted a dark gap, a crack beneath a boulder just large enough in which to hide. Her furry, speckled body disappeared right before the eagle's outstretched claws!

The eagle, its fierce eyes intent only on the chipmunk, hovered above the crack and beat its heavy wings furiously. Frustrated, it scratched the boulder madly and screeched!

Just then, the wolf, seeing only that the chipmunk disappeared behind a large boulder, leapt over the rock, and crashed headlong into the enraged eagle!

A ball of feathers, gray hair, growls, shrieks, claws, and fangs exploded in the cold mountain air. The tangle of ripping, tearing confusion rolled down the hill, past Pappo and Mook, over the crest, and disappeared from view. Their angry screams and growls echoed in the steep ravine below. Then all was silent.

Pappo shook his head, stunned at the turn of events. He wondered what happened and hoped one beast ate the other. Then he saw a gray tail streak into the trees. A winged shadow swiftly slid up a granite wall and flew erratically away.

"The biters! The biters!" Mook screamed to an empty sky.

"Whisper!" Pappo shouted into the crevice where the chipmunk disappeared. "Oh, please tell me you're all right! Whisper!"

Two twitching, tufted ears peeked above the edge of the dark hole followed by shivering whiskers and a trembling, speckled body. Whisper popped out. Suspiciously, she searched the sky and rocks for any danger. Then she skipped quickly downhill and hid in the skinny shadow behind Pappo's thin body. Pappo twisted around to stroke her fur and calm her shivers.

"Save the babes! The biters are coming!" shrieked Mook to no one.

Irritated with Mook's mindless hysterics, Pappo finally yelled at him, "Mook! Stop screaming! There are no biters for moon's sake!"

Mook yelled back at him, "Moon! Moon! Star! Star! Moon!"

"Oh, just great, now see what I started!" Pappo cried out, utterly exasperated. "Whisper, please help me get him to the Long Ice before he starts screaming at the sun!" Pappo stomped irritably over to Mook.

Whisper suddenly squealed and jumped straight up into the air! A long, shiny centipede scurried over the rocks near Mook. Whisper's paws slammed down on it at once. The centipede's green juices bled all over the flat rock. As it lay dying, it wriggled its hundred legs at once then finally wilted away. Whisper looked very satisfied with herself. She wiped her paws in the dust and sniffed the centipede to be sure it was smashed dead.

"Oh! So that was what he was yelling about," exclaimed Pappo, relieved. "Good work, Whisper!

Mook can rest now. You've saved us from a terrifying biter!" he said wryly.

Whisper ruffled her fur, licked her torn patches, and eyed the sick Twig. Resigning herself to carrying him once more, she turned to allow Pappo to lift Mook and the cradle onto her freckled back. Pappo fastened the ropes securely.

Pappo tugged at Whisper's leash and told her, "It's not far now, Whisper. See? There's the Long Ice just up there. When we get there, we'll pack him in the ice and the cold will make him well. Look over there! A straggly, old whitebark pine is still living up here. We can hide in it while Mook gets well. It's not far now, dear, brave Whisper."

They struggled uphill through the sliding rocks until Pappo and Whisper finally stood at the edge of the Long Ice. A vast mass of sparkling white, ancient ice stretched across the mountain as far as they could see. High on Echo Peak, it endured—frozen, gigantic, and silent on the barren, rocky ridge.

Pappo laid Mook gently on the crust of the snow and packed him up to his nose in the ice.

Nearby, the old whitebark pine tree beckoned the exhausted Pappo and weary chipmunk with its knotted, wandering limbs. Its trunk twisted around and around as if it had wrestled with a bitter, stiff wind for so long that the tree's creation could no longer be remembered. Its sparse needles were clumped together like bristly hair, and they smelled sweet. The lovely scent promised soothing dreams to Pappo and Whisper. Its smooth, white bark blended into the peak's drifting mist. The tree was an eerie, lone sentinel at the edge of the massive Long Ice.

Pappo and Whisper sat awake in the whitebark pine a long time to see if Mook would survive the terrible brittlebark disease, but eventually they fell asleep.

Mook suffered quietly now—a freezing lump in the snow. Only the frigid embrace of the Long Ice could heal the sick, old Twig.

CHAPTER EIGHT

THE TOOLER ROUTE

Leaf crouched warily in the roots of a cappynut tree and searched the meadow for Pesky but the tooler was nowhere to be seen. He stood up, pressed his stick body against the scratchy bark of the trunk, narrowed his eyes as if they were thin leaves, and tried to be invisible. He searched the sky but still no Pesky. He needed to search farther from the meadow, but he didn't want to get lost in this strange place either. Leaf hoped the tooler had only wandered away on a bug hunt and might come back to the meadow, if he waited.

Then Leaf heard a merry whistle! It sounded like Pesky but the whistle came from deep in the forest. *Where was he?* Leaf saw a narrow path winding among the trees. It seemed to lead in the direction he heard Pesky. *Might as well follow it*, he decided.

Leaf quickly trotted down the path into the cool shade of the forest. He knew the path was made by delicate hooves—probably by deer which used the trail to the pond to drink its cool water. These graceful creatures usually slept in the heat of the day, so he didn't worry he'd find one on the path now. He hurried along, wondering if he should shout out to Pesky. But that could be dangerous for them both. No need to attract the attention of a red fox or hawk just now.

Abruptly, the pathway died out under a small bluff covered by long, curling strands of grass. The deer could easily leap up and over the bluff, but not Leaf. The path probably continued on, but Leaf would need to find a way up and over.

He heard Pesky whistle again. It seemed nearer this time. *Good*, he thought. *At least I'm moving in the right direction!*

A huckleberry bush grew against the bluff, so Leaf crawled into its twisted branches. After a sticky, scratchy climb, he stood on top of a downward sloping hill, once again in the middle of the deer path. The flickering sunbeams in the trees made him feel uneasy. There were so many silent birds rustling overhead in the branches as if they watched and waited in fear. Leaf knew birds were only quiet if a hunter prowled the woods or circled in the sky. He must be very cautious.

Very worried now, it also occurred to him that perhaps another tooler had called, not Pesky. Perhaps he was following the wrong trail after all. He suddenly realized he might run on this path all day and never find Pesky. Leaf knew this was no way to find the tooler!

He stopped abruptly and stood with his hands on his hips in the middle of the sunny path, considering his choices. He could keep running and hope he found Pesky somewhere in the woods, or maybe a better plan might be to bring Pesky to him. Perhaps the silly tooler would return if he played a song on his whistletube. *After all, he might think I have berries for him.* There was hardly any choice left to him at all, Leaf realized. He must try to bring Pesky to him.

Leaf ducked into the cover of a hemlock's knotty roots and drew out the whistletube. Soon a sweet melody drifted up through the heavy branches of the red cedar and hemlock trees.

Immediately, an answering whistle sang back.

It's working, Leaf thought! *If that's Pesky, he will come to me.*

But Pesky didn't.

Leaf played a long time, but the tooler did not come. Every once in a while, Leaf heard a tooler calling and he believed it must be Pesky. His cheery whistle seemed to come from some place farther down the trail.

Perhaps he's stuck somewhere? Leaf wondered about this. Still, Pesky's whistle didn't sound as if he were calling for help. *Why doesn't he come to me? Well, it is time to get up and find him!* Leaf ran swiftly down the path again, very disturbed.

The trail suddenly ended at the stump of a huge tree that rose upended from the earth. Huge clumps of mud and dead roots stuck out of it. Mushrooms and ferns grew in clumps from torn pieces of dangling bark. Leaf stared at it and wondered if Pesky was trapped inside this muddy tangle.

Dirt and pebbles suddenly dribbled onto Leaf's green leafy head. He looked up. Pesky hopped happily about on top of the massive, fallen tree. With his sharp claws, he scratched loose more of the dried mud and made Leaf jump back to avoid the tumbling dirt and dead leaves.

"Stop it, Pesky! For moon's sake, what are you doing up there?" Leaf said irritably.

The tooler just hopped around and looked very pleased to see his new Twig friend. He strutted back and forth then disappeared. Evidently he must have walked farther down the trunk from the upended bottom, guessed Leaf.

"Pesky, stop!" cried Leaf. "We have to fly north. This is no time to scratch around for worms in the rotten wood! Please, Pesky, come back!" But Pesky did not.

Well, great, thought Leaf. *Now I'll need to climb up after him.* He scrambled up the dead roots sticking out at odd angles, and quickly pulled himself up on the log where Pesky had kicked the dirt in his hair.

Then he froze, shocked at what he saw. A mighty chasm fell away before him. A deep sickening cut in the granite of the forest floor divided the South Forest from the North Forest. The gigantic roots of the log lay half-buried on the south side of the gorge. Its massive trunk extended out high above a river flowing far below. The winding river looked like a thin blue ribbon from this dizzying height. The dead tree's top branches clutched tightly to granite slabs sticking out from the sheer cliff at the north edge of the chasm.

Leaf realized the chasm was twice as deep as the Old Seeder was tall. He gazed at the terrifying drop below him. The cliff walls were far too steep for Twigs or creatures to climb.

Leaf understood at once. *The old log is a bridge over the chasm! If Pesky cannot carry all of us when we return, then this log bridge is the only way back across. Pesky must have seen this tree when he flew to our forest. He is showing me the only way back.* At that moment, Leaf knew for sure there *were* Twigs trapped in the North Forest. He must find them and bring them back across this log.

"Thank you, Pesky!" Leaf cried out. "Now we have a way back home!"

Pesky hopped up and down, excited his friend finally understood.

Leaf looked around to get his bearings. On the other side of the gorge, two towering sugar pine trees grew. They were very tall. At their base, the trunk was actually one, but it had split into two separate trees. The trunks grew parallel to each other, providing support to each other, yet separate. This tree was unusual enough to be a marker from far away. If Leaf could see the sugar pine trees, he could find the log bridge.

Leaf also noticed the trees were brown in the North Forest. *How strange!* He puzzled over the distressing sight. The trees appeared to be dying or already dead! *It couldn't be!* Leaf shook his head in disbelief. But there was no time to figure it out. It was time to continue the journey.

"All right, Pesky. We can fly now," Leaf told him. "Take me straight from here to Mook's Star haven. I'll watch the route you fly. No need to waste time. We'll bring any Twigs there right back to this bridge. Good job, Pesky! You're a brilliant tooler!" Leaf stroked the luminescent feathers on Pesky's neck and smiled. He wouldn't need to go back for Pappo's help after all! Pesky had shown him the route to take back to the Old Seeder. All he needed to do now was find Mook's Twigs. Leaf grinned. *With Pesky's help, I'll bring them back to the South Forest all by myself!*

Leaf gazed at the unbelievably deep chasm under the trunk of the tree bridge. He scanned each side of the gorge and saw there were no other crossing points farther up or down the gorge. Either you were in the North Forest, or you were in the South. The gorge divided the two. If this old tree had not fallen here, or had not fallen just the way it did, no wingless creature would be able to cross over this awesome crack in the earth.

Leaf felt dizzy. He steadied his shaky legs and pressed his face into Pesky's feathers. He grabbed the rope around the tooler's neck, glad to spring onto his back once more.

Pesky skipped a little, hopped once, then he launched himself off the broad trunk and into the wide canyon. The tooler flapped his strong wings until he caught a draft of air racing up from the canyon floor. With Leaf clinging gratefully to the golden braid, Pesky soared high above the forest and once more flew north.

When Leaf gained enough courage to peek out from the tooler's feathers, they were already flying over the sugar pine trees, and away from the steep cliffs of the gorge.

Pesky searched the sky for danger.

Leaf looked down and saw only dying trees—their pale, brittle limbs stretched to each other like ghostly arms searching for help. Leaf shivered.

CHAPTER NINE

THE STICKYTOES AND LOOKSALOT

Star walked slowly alongside Veil to the other side of the cave. Veil, Click, Chirp, and Crunch were a strong defense against barkbiters. Their quick-lashing tongues protected the babes, Moon, and Star as long as the Twigs remained in the cave. Moon and Star had also covered the entrance with sticky, abandoned spider webs which had been left hanging in the dying trees. Even barkbiters avoided webs. Their short, stubby legs were too slow for the swift, poisonous spiders.

Veil stepped away from the web as if he were very tired. His tail usually curled up in a spiral but now it dragged on the ground. He rocked back and forth unsteadily with each step he took. The broad gold and blue stripes that circled his thick body pulsated as he moved from light to shadow. Finally, Veil changed color completely to a murky dark brown and tan.

Star, Moon, and the stickytoes were very patient with Veil. He more than made up for his slow motion with his incredibly long, stretchy tongue. His ability to strike a bug from far away was astonishing. Barkbiters never came near the unusual creature. Even as a young looksalot, his whipping tongue made up for his inability to move quickly. Veil was a perfect looksalot.

Star found Veil stuck inside a rotting knothole when he was no longer than her own skinny finger. She was only five seasons old then. Star had been exploring along a marshy creek. An old, twisted tree had fallen and lay crumbling on the creek bank, its hollow trunk half-exposed, one of its old knotholes still intact. That was the day she discovered Veil.

Star was always curious about bugs. She liked to uncover their hiding places. So she peeked into the dark knothole. A flicker of light pierced the shadows. Star heard strange scratching noises and chirping calls from within, so she knelt down and looked more closely. The light was dim but Star could just make out three orange-spotted, newborn stickytoes. Curled up beside them, a weird looking creature lay motionless. It was slightly larger than the stickytoes, pale green, and Star knew at once, it was not a common creature of the North Forest at all. She recognized it from the stories her mums told. A looksalot had found its way into the soft, rotting nest of the stickytoes! Star was fascinated with her discovery. She watched as the newborn stickytoes nuzzled fluff into a ball and tugged tiny sticks around them to arrange their cluttered nest. With weird rolling eyes, the looksalot lay absolutely still, and watched the stickytoes fuss around in the knothole.

Star wondered often since that day how a looksalot could have possibly come to the North Forest. They did not live in the cool air naturally, so perhaps he was dropped by a bird lost in the fog. Maybe the bird had snatched the looksalot up from his faraway nest, but decided the tiny creature was too strange to eat after all, and dropped him here, into the stickytoes' knothole.

In any case, when Star saw the tiny brood together, she knew she should not bother them, yet she returned many times over the next few days to peek at them again. They chirped and scrunched around in their nest as Star watched, mesmerized. The stickytoes crawled quickly and skillfully, racing after bugs, and gulping them down. But the looksalot simply sat, watched for bugs with his odd rolling eyes, and waited for a chance to fling out his long, pink tongue to snap one up.

The first time Star saw the looksalot snatch a tiny bug from the rim of the knothole, she was startled and fell backwards, astonished. His tongue was impossibly long!

Sadly, it was not long before Star noticed the four tiny creatures were becoming weaker and sluggish instead of stronger. She soon realized their mum was not caring for them, no longer coming to the nest. Perhaps the looksalot frightened her away. He moved so slowly, it was almost painful to watch, and his eyes . . . well, his eyes *were* spooky.

To help out, Star caught some worms for the brood. Soon she brought them food many times during the day. Surprisingly, the stickytoes and looksalot were not yet precise with their tongues. It took a great deal of practice for them to feed themselves. Many bugs got away. Star knocked them back into the nest whenever they tried to flee the knothole. The stickytoes' tongues did not have the incredible reach of the looksalot's, but they were enthusiastic hunters. Their flat mouths smiled eternally even as they gulped down the frantically kicking, struggling bugs. The stickytoes evidently had a great deal of respect for the looksalot, because they waited patiently for their strange companion to snatch his meal before they grabbed their own. It was a funny little family, but they seemed loyal to each other.

Star named the stickytoes after their sweet chirps, clicks, and crunchy noises they made eating bugs. But it took some time for her to name the looksalot. Finally she named him Veil because of his shy, reclusive nature and weird way of changing colors. He probably would have preferred to remain behind a veil and hide in the shadows, but his stickytoes friends were playful company. Often they chased bugs near Veil just to watch him snatch one. Soon Veil was a chubby looksalot.

Later, they expected Star to arrive with food in hand. They crawled to her, and allowed Star to hold them in her palm and kiss them on their noses. The cheerful stickytoes and thoughtful looksalot loved her madly. Before long they grew old enough for Star to carry them around. The curious creatures climbed all over Star, poked their noses in her silver, leafy hair, and perched on her slender shoulders. She took them walking in the forest. The stickytoes were allowed to sit happily on her head and shoulders, but she always cupped Veil protectively in her hands. It was not long before her sweet, curious friends went with her everywhere.

Star remembered when she first saw her dear stickytoes swim. They were all out for a little stroll together along a sunny forest path when suddenly Chirp, Crunch, and Click jumped from her shoulders and disappeared into wet leaves on the side of the pathway. Star peered into the shadows of the woods. Where had the stickytoes gone? She had no choice but to follow their rustling sounds—already far from where she stood. She plunged through the hanging ivy vines, still protecting Veil, who crouched in her hands. Thorny brambles stuck to her leafy head and grabbed at her feet, yet she moved as quickly as possible in the direction of the rustling leaves, fearful of losing her precious friends. Finally she skidded into a small sunlit glade. A shallow, sparkling pond spread out before her. Pretty blue periwinkles and pink daisies flowed over the pond's edges. Colorful stones lay on its green mossy bottom and shimmered in the clear water.

Then she saw them. Click, Chirp, and Crunch sat blissfully *under* the water on round, mossy rocks. Star had no idea that stickytoes could naturally hold their breath for a long time. She watched, awestruck. Click, Chirp, and Crunch studied the waving plants before them with huge brown eyes. They darted up from the pond's depths, and caught long-legged lake flies that squatted on the pond's surface. Star was mesmerized with their water play and watched them maneuver skillfully underwater all day. Veil sat and waited patiently in her hand.

As they grew older, the looksalot and the three stickytoes grew too big to carry. Chirp, Crunch, and Click now gave Star rides on their slippery backs. She giggled and slid off when they raced each other up trees to tackle a bug.

Veil was too delicate for such antics. He would find a perch and guard the merry group from danger—like the time a horde of vicious hornets appeared. Veil's powerful tongue shot out instantly, and he crushed many of them in his flat mouth. Stunned at the ferocity of the looksalot's attack, the hornets whirled off in a confused jumble into the forest. Nothing threatened Star or the stickytoes when Veil was nearby.

Star stroked Veil's soft scales and laughed to herself, remembering the time she stumbled into a red ant bed.

The ants were huge—as large as Star's hands. In one frightening moment, the furious ants attacked and surrounded her in a fiery crimson ring. But the ants were no match for the flashing tongues of the stickytoes and looksalot. Not one red ant stung Star, although she stood in the middle of hundreds. The stickytoes' tongues struck fast and furiously. The looksalot's tongue shot out straight across the red ant bed and pulled back dozens of the nasty creatures at once. At last the red ant leader gave an invisible, silent signal, and the mass of wriggling, crimson attackers fled into the forest. That day, a grand meal of crunchy red ants filled the bellies of the stickytoes and looksalot.

Star knew that her odd friends would always protect her without hesitation. She never doubted their fierce loyalty. Crunch, Chirp, Click, and Veil had no doubts of Star's devotion to them either.

When the barkbiters came to the North Forest, the ugly, evil creatures steered clear of the dangerous, crushing tongues of Veil and the stickytoes. Yet, even with this remarkable defense, Star worried about her dear creatures when they tramped about in the trees. So she fashioned light shields for them from soft bark and smooth stones. She placed the shields across their shoulders and on their heads. She strapped them on with flaxen braids under their smooth bellies.

Click, Chirp, and Crunch were very proud of their tough-looking appearance and guarded the Twigs even more earnestly. Sometimes, they'd puff themselves up to twice their size, and appear even more fearsome.

Sometimes Click and Chirp would silently creep up on Moon, and steal his short, stabbing spear and curved rock shard. They would prance back and forth in the cave merrily flourishing their stolen weapons. Crunch, who was very fond of Moon, simply shook the loose, scarlet skin below his chin in irritation.

Although Moon could not catch the mischievous Click and Chirp, he chased them around the cave and tried to snatch back his precious hunting tools. The stickytoes simply scaled the rock walls and hung from the ceiling, teasing Moon, and grinning at him. Eventually, Moon gave up and simply let them carry his spear and shard with them whenever they left the cave to stalk the forest.

Now that the Twigs were forced to hide in the cave, Star depended on her bizarre friends to bring food and water to them every day. Even when the stickytoes came back to the cave, they hardly rested before leaving again to find food. Star wondered how long the stickytoes and Veil would be able to continue looking after them this way.

She patted Veil's nose as he stepped onto his sleeping rock. Carefully and slowly, the looksalot coiled his long tail into a spiral beside him. Star glanced over her shoulder and checked on Chirp, Crunch, and Click. They lay in a row, flat on their bellies, and faced the sticky web. Nothing would enter the cave while the stickytoes were on guard. Even if Click, Crunch, or Chirp occasionally napped, any vibrations they felt in the clay earth would alert them in an instant.

Star knew they were safe for one more night. The barkbiters had not found them...yet.

CHAPTER TEN

LEAF MEETS STAR

Leaf and Pesky flew north during the mist of mid-morning. Cold rain drizzled on them. Beads of icy water dribbled down Pesky's dark wings. Clear, crystal drops soaked Leaf. Pesky flew just above a sharp ridge of granite which peeked out from a lake of thick fog. The fog hung halfway down the ridge and smothered all but the highest brown tips of the pine trees which surrounded the steep, gray cliffs.

Leaf watched their path carefully. If for some reason Pesky left him stranded in the North Forest, Leaf would need to find his own way back to the sugar pines by the log bridge. The ridgeline was crooked and steep but it continually ran southward. *The ridge will be a good guide back*, Leaf assured himself.

Pesky used the rocky crest as a guide, too. Whenever the fog drifted higher and covered the jagged cliffs from view, Pesky glided fearlessly down into the mist to keep the ridgeline in sight. But now Pesky flew even higher. The foggy cloud was far below and the ridge could be easily seen. The rain drizzled less and the fog thinned slightly in the bright sun.

Suddenly Pesky tilted sideways, his wings stretched out wide to catch a downward draft. He spiraled slowly until he swooped into the tree tops and down into the fog. He dropped his wings a little and slowed even more. Then the tooler banked left, then right. He studied the trees and boulders in the thick fog bank with black, piercing eyes as if searching for some special place.

Leaf peered through the murky fog but saw nothing. He wondered what drew Pesky here.

Abruptly, Pesky's wings beat the air furiously. He hovered above a large, flat slab. At once, Pesky plummeted down, and clumsily skipped to a stop on top of the rock. With an annoyed shudder, he shook Leaf from his back.

Leaf plopped onto the slab with a loud grunt.

Immediately, Pesky whirled around and poked Leaf in the back with his beak, nearly stabbing him right through his strap. With a low whistle, Pesky rudely shoved Leaf toward the edge of the massive rock.

Leaf dug his heels hard into the cracks in the granite to keep from being pushed over the edge. "Stop it!" cried Leaf.

Pesky just kept shoving him.

Fine, gray dust swirled around Leaf as he pushed back against the tooler's insistent beak. "Stop it! Leave me alone, Pesky!" Leaf shouted as he spit out some dirt.

Pesky stepped back from Leaf, shook his head at the stubborn Twig, and flew away.

"Oh, come on!" Leaf cried after him. "I didn't mean go away!" Now exasperated, Leaf called after him, "Come back, Pesky! Oh, come back!" Leaf stood up and brushed the dirt from his hair and arms. A gray cloud rose up around him and floated away. Leaf stared for a long time into the thick fog where Pesky had disappeared. He waited and waited then he realized the tooler was not going to return any time soon. "Just great," he muttered, "just great!"

Cautiously, Leaf slid half way down the boulder, and jumped to the muddy earth below. A steamy mist floated all around Leaf, clung to the trees, and suffocated their dry fronds. Leaf stuck out his finger and spun a fat circle in the fog. Laughing to himself, he looked through the circle's center. The circle spun wider and wider. Finally, it floated away on gray ripples. At last, it tore apart before a dark, cavernous hole at the base of the massive boulder.

It was an entrance to a cave!

In disbelief, Leaf waved away the fog and looked again. Shielding the shadowy entrance to the cave were gobs of spider webs. Leaf suddenly felt very uneasy. This creepy place was just like his dream! He shivered in the cold, damp air. In his ears, he seemed to hear Buddy and Burba's giggles from far away. He seemed to feel the warm sun streaming through fragrant, green leaves by the Old Seeder's creek. This place looked just like the same cave he had dreamed about, but this time he was awake. Leaf stood silent, afraid to move.

Leaf remembered then that Pesky brought had him to this place. This *must* be Star haven where the Twig babes were stranded. This dark cave had to be a hiding place. Leaf knew he must search the dark hole no matter how frightened he felt.

Cautiously, he stepped near the webs. He froze. Something large moved slowly behind the silken threads. Now Leaf really felt nervous. Intently, he peered through the web into the cave.

Just then, sunbeams broke through the fog, brilliant and hot. Puddles of rainbows lay all around Leaf. He took a deep breath, shrugged off his uneasy feelings, and drew his saver from the loop on his back. Stepping forward, he parted the web with the stone end of his saver and told himself to simply ignore how creepy it all was. He stabbed the walking stick into the dirt between his feet. Slowly Leaf turned the saver until its pale blue stone caught a bright ray of sun. An intense, bluish, blast of light shot out, bounced into the cave, and pierced the dark shadows. Leaf held the light steady, leaned forward, and stared into the cave.

Stars. He saw stars. There were stars shining in the dark. Leaf felt cold. He wanted to turn and run away, but he knew he must find out if Mook's dream talk was true. He puzzled over seeing stars in the depths of a cave. As he stared at them, they blinked! Shocked, Leaf realized that they were not stars at all! *They were white, glimmering eyes staring back up at him! White eyes!*

Leaf sucked in a sharp, ragged breath. The leaves on his head trembled.

Then a soft, cool voice spoke from the darkness. "Are you here to rescue us?" A young Twig with silver, leafy hair stepped into the beam of blue light and blinked quickly. "Well, are you coming in? You really should drop the web, you know."

Without thinking, Leaf pushed the web even further back with the saver, and stepped inside. Realizing what he had done, he hastily disentangled his saver from the spider web, and dropped the sticky glob behind him. He stuttered, unsure of himself for some reason. "Is this, uh, Star haven? Pesky, uh, I mean a tooler brought me here. Mook, uh, I mean an old Twig said there were, uh, Twig babes stranded somewhere."

"PapaMook! PapaMook!" Suddenly tiny chirping voices cried out excitedly. "Did you bring PapaMook back? Where's PapaMook?" Small Twig bodies rushed around in the dim light.

"No, I've come alone," Leaf explained, turning toward the twittering noises. He saw many Twig babe faces staring up at him, disappointed. They began to sniffle and cry.

"Where's PapaMook?" they peeped.

Leaf tried to calm their worries. "He's with my Pappo," he answered kindly. "He was sick, so my Pappo took him to the Long Ice to get well. He'll be all right. But he couldn't travel. So I came." Still, Leaf felt his words were insufficient and lame.

For the first time since he stepped inside the cavern, Leaf noticed a large creature, nearly motionless, sitting by the webs. His eyes rolled in different directions and he held a two-toed hand up in the air, frozen, as if he were surprised. Leaf stared at the bizarre creature, and tried to remember the old Twig adventure stories Mumma had told him. She had described strange living things from other places in the world. Leaf realized this odd creature must be a looksalot! But how could a looksalot come to live in the North Forest? Leaf stared at the weird creature which stared back at him with one bulging eye.

"So, you're here by yourself?" a new Twig voice spoke. A sour-looking Twig stepped over to stand beside the silver-haired Twig who spoke before. He was taller than her. Both gazed at Leaf with cool, pale eyes and skeptical expressions. "No more Twigs came to help?"

Leaf knew at once they were brother and sister. They resembled each other so very closely. "Yes," he answered. "I've come to take you to my home."

"Right . . ." The tall Twig's voice trailed off.

Leaf began to wonder why they weren't glad to see him. Perhaps he just needed to explain his plan. "I know the way back to my forest. I can take you there," he assured them. "Pesky flew above a ridge that can guide us south."

The soft-voiced Twig raised her hand to stop Leaf from speaking any further. "Who are you?"

"Oh," replied Leaf. "I'm Leaf of the Old Seeder Twigs." Then he added, "This is Star haven, right? You all need a guide, right?"

The silver-haired Twig smiled wryly. The tall, sour Twig frowned at Leaf. "Well," she spoke, "I'm Star. This is my brother, Moon. These babes are in our care. This is Sand, Moss, Breeze, Cone, Mist, and Pool." She paused to hush their sad whimpers then turned back to Leaf. "And we didn't need a guide. We needed guards."

"But there's no need for guards," Leaf explained patiently. "I know the way back. There's a log over the gorge. We can cross to my forest there." At last feeling more confident, Leaf stood straight and gripped his saver as if he were in charge of an unruly Twig mob. "We should leave at once. We have half a day still and we can get pretty far by nightfall." Leaf grinned as he imagined Pappo's face. He wanted to return to the Old Seeder before his Pappo did.

Star shook her head sadly. Moon actually appeared angry. He simply glowered at Leaf with disturbing, white eyes. The babes sat silent, now knowing something was very wrong. They listened intently to the older Twigs talk.

Leaf noticed for the first time how pale Star and Moon's woody faces were. *Is there any color at all in this north land?* he wondered. *How long have they been in this dismal cave? Why are they all so reluctant to leave?* Annoyed by their silence, Leaf pushed on with his plan and asked, "Do you have enough food for a trip? How about water?"

Moon snorted in disgust, "How about a hundred Peskys to carry us away?"

Leaf stared at him, totally confused. *What is wrong with these Twigs?*

Star waved a hand at Moon to quiet him. Then she spoke to Leaf in a low voice. "Leaf, didn't you notice our trees are dying?"

Leaf nodded, even more confused.

Star said sadly, "Leaf, we're surrounded by barkbiters. We can't escape through the forest." She looked puzzled at his blank expression. "Haven't you heard of barkbiters?"

"Yes, I noticed the trees," Leaf answered irritably. "No, I haven't heard of, uh, biters."

"*Barkbiters*, I said," continued Star with a stern voice. "They are the reason our trees are brown. They are the reason the babes have no family to protect them. They are the reason we hide in this cave. They are the reason we cannot leave here without guards. We need guards with hunting tools that can kill barkbiters when they attack." Star spoke slowly and calmly, as if to a naive babe. But now her voice began to tremble and her words rushed out. "Leaf, we have so little time. Soon the barkbiters will find our cave. When they do, we will not get out of here alive!"

The Twig babes began to sniffle again. Star knelt down and embraced as many as she could to comfort them.

Leaf began to feel sick. What were these awful creatures . . . barkbiters? And what had he gotten himself into? Then suddenly he realized Pappo would come looking for him. Pappo would come for him and walk right into this deadly forest! Instantly, Leaf knew that he must go back and warn his family. Even worse, these barkbiters might find the log that crossed over the gorge! If they found the log bridge, they could find the Old Seeder!

Leaf felt like running away, but he hesitated. He couldn't just leave these Twigs alone here either. Leaf stood very still, considering what he should do. Then he knew. He must get them all safely to the log as soon as possible. And they must reach it before Pappo crossed over!

They must leave now!

CHAPTER ELEVEN

MY STICKYTOES!

Now Leaf was very worried about Pappo. Star, Moon, and the Twig babes must leave at once.

"We need to leave now," Leaf said firmly. "My Pappo will come here to search for me. If Mook is still dream talking, Pappo will not know about the barkbiters. We must reach the log before he comes to your forest." Leaf paused. "The day's not flowing any slower!" he added his family saying to encourage them.

Moon stood very still. Hope flickered in his eyes. "So what do we do about the barkbiters, Leaf?"

Star looked back and forth in disbelief at Moon and Leaf. "We can't leave the cave!" she cried out. "You can't be serious!"

Leaf stared directly into Moon's white eyes. "Moon, you must fly back on Pesky and warn Pappo about the danger in your forest. You must leave now. Star and I will lead the babes through the forest. If we move fast, I can guard them!" Leaf jammed his saver into the ground like a hunter to emphasize his words.

"But what about at night...what if they come at night?" Star said, her voice trembling.

"We will hide in the rocks and caves along the ridge, high up away from the trees, just like you hide here in this cave. Does your looksalot protect you here at night?" Leaf asked.

Suddenly alarmed, Star shouted, "My stickytoes!"

Startled, Leaf stared down at Star's toes. They were dark brown and curly like any other Twig's toes. He looked up at Star, puzzled with her sudden outburst. He studied her toes again.

Star looked terribly distressed and cried out again, "My stickytoes!"

"Your toes?" Leaf asked, feeling very confused. "Your sticky toes?"

Star wondered why Leaf stared at her feet. She forced herself to calm down and, with a condescending tone in her voice, explained, "My stickytoes are on the island gathering food. They come back at twilight when barkbiters are not so active. We must go get them!"

"Oh, yes, stickytoes!" Leaf answered blankly. He was still confused. Whatever stickytoes were, they must be important and certainly seemed helpful. "Um, can the babes ride the stickytoes?"

Unexpectedly, Moon clapped his hand together. "Of course!" Moon exclaimed. "Right! Good idea! The babes can ride the stickytoes!" Then he glanced at the motionless looksalot, and paused. "You'll have to pull Veil on a sled, though."

Leaf gazed doubtfully at the large creature by the spider webs.

Moon looked a little sheepish. "Uh, he's pretty slow when it comes to walking."

"Yes! Good idea!" Star exclaimed. Her expression brightened at once. She shook her head up and down vehemently. "We can do this! Moon, while we go get the stickytoes, gather up all our braided ropes. We've made so many braids while we waited for PapaMook." She motioned to a lumpy pile of hand-woven baskets and ropes braided from gold flax. "And use the spider webs, too, to make padded cradles so the babes can ride on Click, Chirp, and Crunch. Then make a sled some-how that will be large enough to pull Veil."

Moon nodded earnestly.

Star stepped over to her younger brother, and placed her slender hands on his shoulders. "Moon," she said, "you will need to fly on Pesky. You must make that silly, stubborn tooler let you to ride him. He has no choice. You must leave as soon as we return from the island. Go find PapaMook and warn Leaf's Pappo." She looked deep into his eyes. "We can stay here no longer. It's time to leave. Perhaps Leaf *will* be able to guide us through the forest safely. In any case, if we become trapped and do not meet you at the log, look for us in the caves on the high ridge."

Moon nodded, very serious. All trace of a sour or sul-len attitude had vanished.

"Be careful, Star," Moon cautioned her as he nodded toward Leaf. "You have little protection out there even if he does have a big stick with a shiny stone."

Star smiled and nodded. She glanced at Leaf then stepped over to a small basket, dug around inside, pulled out some crumpled leaves, and tossed them at Leaf's feet. "Here. Slip these on. The needles are so brittle they'll pierce your feet if you aren't wearing these tough ivy leaves." Star hastily tugged on her own worn-out ivy slippers and moved at once to the spider web. She lifted it slightly, and slid through. She spoke softly over her shoulder to Leaf, "You coming?" and dropped the web before Leaf could reach her.

Leaf was still trying to figure out who Click, Chirp, and Crunch were. But he shook his head to clear his thoughts, tugged on the rubbery, thick, ivy slippers, and moved quickly to follow Star. He pushed aside the web and caught sight of Star's shadow disappearing among dry, brown pine trees. She had taken a very narrow unused deer path through a pile of crackling, stiff needles. The forest floor was covered with prickly cones which had fallen from the dying limbs.

Leaf caught up to Star quickly. Abruptly, she spun around to face him, her finger to her lips, and he nearly slid into her. She glared at him. In a voice barely audible, she whispered urgently, "Silence! Be very quiet, Leaf. Make no sound!" The needles barely rustled as she silently and skillfully sprinted off down the trail.

Leaf nodded sharply, annoyed. *Well, who does she think she's talking to? He knew how to blend into trees, to be invisible, and he could certainly move without making any noise!* He ran after her, his steps deathly quiet, and matched his pace to hers. He considered the back of Star's leafy head. *This rude Twig isn't the only one who can be silent on a deer trail.*

Star and Leaf trotted along the thin, winding path for a long while. Thorny cones hid beneath the needles, so Leaf was grateful for the slippers. The ancient trees rose, rigid, against an amazingly clear blue sky. Occasionally, annoying gnats buzzed at them and angrily flew at their eyes. Leaf batted them away. Sometimes, white butterflies floated randomly in the oddly still air. They seemed sad and lost in the patchy shadows. It was eerie. Leaf felt as if some danger crept around him, but he couldn't see it. He felt jumpy and nervous.

Star never slowed her pace. She led him through the forest without a word and never looked back to see if Leaf followed or not. Her shoulders were stiff and her stride was determined. Leaf knew she needed to find her stickytoes—whatever they were.

Finally Star ducked into the large, tangled roots of an old cedar tree which stood sentinel on the edge of a sapphire-colored lake. Leaf dropped into the roots beside her and gazed at the beautiful, smooth water. *There is still some beauty here*, he thought.

Dusty trees ringed the lake which mirrored a startling, crystal-like sky. In the middle of the lake there was an island where towering pine trees grew. Amazingly, the trees on the island were still an emerald green and healthy. Leaf gripped the coolness of damp moss between his stick fingers. At least the moss still continued to grow in the roots, too. Even so, there was very little life here.

Leaf glanced behind him and wondered if the barkbiters could swim. *Or perhaps they just hadn't bothered to try.*

Star pointed furtively from the safety of the roots toward the island. "They are over there," she whispered in a low voice. "They go there every day and gather seeds, nuts, and grass for us to eat."

"You eat grass?" asked Leaf, and he almost laughed. Immediately Leaf wished he hadn't said anything at all.

Star looked embarrassed. "Try it sometime," she said angrily.

"I'm sorry," Leaf whispered. He truly regretted his thoughtless words. "I'm sure it's been very hard to survive here."

Star was a little mollified and her eyes softened. She turned and gazed thoughtfully at the green island.

Finally she sighed. "I don't know how to get their attention without alerting the barkbiters. If we swim . . ." her voice sank away as she pointed to the sky.

Leaf looked up. Three enormous eagles slowly circled overhead, searching for movement on the earth and in the lake below. *Well, that's a relief,* Leaf thought at once, *since I can't swim anyway.* He glanced at Star, wondering if she saw his expression.

Leaf considered the lakeshore which was littered with rocks and splinters sticking in the mud. Except for the lake's shallow ripples splashing against the dead logs which lined the edge, all was deathly quiet. *We can't just sit here all day,* Leaf worried. *We must get to the island and find these stickytoes. We can't just wait for them to look for us!*

All at once, a mighty shudder shook the ground beneath Leaf's feet. Startled, Leaf searched the forest behind them and caught a glimpse of a gigantic moose as it lumbered its way through low-hanging, dead branches. It knocked thin limbs from the trees and stumbled over logs with huge, heavy hooves. Massive antlers grew out of its incredibly broad head. Its velvet nose snorted and blew hot mist into the air as it gracelessly dropped its hooves, crushing one fallen limb after another. The moose's eyes were very tiny black beads in its long, drooping face. They were fairly useless. Nearly blind, it relied on birds to guide it to water and followed their song to the meadow to nibble grass.

Actually it was a very gentle beast. Still, all things fled hastily before its colossal, swaying body and lurching movements. Finally it made its way to the lake and waded up to its huge, knobby knees. Slowly it lowered its giant head to daintily sip the icy water with large, flapping lips.

Leaf placed his hand on Star's arm. "That's it," he said flatly. Immediately he pulled clumps of moss from under the tree. He rolled the moss clumps into a fat ball then scrambled over the tree's twisted roots and grabbed a long, willowy stick.

Star stared at him in disbelief. "What are you doing?" she whispered incredulously.

Leaf waved at her, begging her silence and patience. Then he crept toward the moose, still happily satisfying its great thirst. Leaf motioned to Star to follow him closely. She crawled from the roots and shadowed his steps.

Even though Leaf was barely as tall as the great brute's knees, the stick he held was longer than its leg. The ball of heavy moss bounced up and down on the end of the stick as Leaf struggled to keep it steady. He crouched down a few paces from the rear end of the moose, took a short run then jumped as high as he could. He landed squarely on the moose's rump! Unaware of Leaf, the moose continued to slurp up water and swish its tail back and forth to shoo away the gnats.

Leaf frantically waved to Star to jump on, too. She made it to the moose's rump but lost her balance for an instant. She grabbed Leaf's arm and he caught her hand. As he pulled her up, he somehow kept hold of the slender stick laden with the ball of moss. They crawled on their hands and knees over the rough hair on the moose's back. Cautiously, they climbed onto its wide, velvet antlers.

The broad back of the moose shivered fiercely for an instant as if it finally felt something creeping on its back and wished to discourage whatever it was from resting on its scratchy, stiff hair.

Leaf swung the long stick out in front of the moose's nose and wiggled the clump of moss just above its snorting nostrils.

The moose grunted, blinked, sniffed the moss, and stepped forward. It took another step, another, and another as it followed the sweet smell of the moss until it was up to its chest in the water. At last it was swimming happily through the frigid water, its powerful legs and desire for the sweet moss taking it to wherever Leaf held the ball of moss.

Leaf guided the gentle, giant beast toward the island. The eagles, which circled high in the sky, glanced at the huge beast swimming below and dismissed it as likely prey.

Star laughed with delight. "Brilliant, Leaf!" She clapped and grinned.

Leaf felt suddenly shy but grinned back. Star and Leaf sat close together on the giant antlers and enjoyed riding the moose as its massive antlers swayed up and down, back and forth. The moose swam steadily through the cold, blue lake.

As they neared the island, Leaf spoke seriously to Star. "You must hurry. I don't know how long this trick will keep it here."

Star nodded. As they neared the island's shore, she slid from the back of the moose, dropped into the shallow water, and splashed her way across to the pebbled beach. Then she raced off immediately into the thickets of the huckleberry bushes lining the lake shore.

Leaf held the moss before the mighty beast's nose and led it around and around in a great circle. He hoped with each breath that Star would soon return with her stickytoes. He searched the bushes on the lake's edge constantly as the moose dog-paddled in the water after the sweet-smelling moss.

How patient this great brute is, Leaf thought. *It follows the moss so serenely, so free from worry. But will it tire of this game soon?* Leaf hoped not.

Finally Leaf heard rustling from the huckleberry bushes. Just as he glanced over, Star burst through, raced toward Leaf, and leaped over the rippling water onto the back of the moose. Coming straight behind her—in a line, nose to tail—three orange-spotted stickytoes crawled from under the bushes. They splashed into the water, swam over to the moose—who was still swimming after the moss—climbed up its tail, and squatted behind Star.

The creatures grinned happily at Leaf with flat, wide mouths. Their curious, deep-brown, wet eyes glimmered sweetly. Each carried a pouch, bound around their middle, half-stuffed with grass, pine nuts, and seeds. They wore soft, bark helmets and shoulder shields.

Leaf stared at them in surprise. Stickytoes! So that's what Star meant. In his forest, these funny-looking creatures were called barkhuggers. Leaf had never seen such brilliant orange spots on barkhuggers or any colors as stunning as these! They were astonishing!

Star grinned at Leaf. She was obviously proud of her stickytoes. "This is Click, Chirp, and Crunch, my sticky-toes!" She motioned to each.

Leaf wondered how she could possibly know the difference between them. They appeared identical. Then he noticed one had a flapping, reddish-colored, hanging chin. One carried a short stabbing spear tucked into his shield. The last of the three had a rock shard shoved in his belt.

"They're beautiful!" Leaf exclaimed. Politely he nodded to each one and said formally, "How do you fare today?"

Star looked sideways at Leaf. "They don't speak, Leaf," she said, exasperated. "But they do understand." Star smiled at them, nearly glowing with love for her stickytoes. "Well, mighty moose leader," she said enthusiastically, "let's go!"

Leaf wiggled the ball of moss before the moose's huge nose. He led it away from the island and back toward the dying forest. Soon they were near the brown trees once more. The mighty beast rose dripping from the lake just as Star and Leaf jumped to a crumbling, log on the lakeshore. The stickytoes slipped from the moose's rump and scuttled silently into the roots of a nearby cedar.

Leaf rewarded the great moose for its help. He lifted the moss to its lips and the moose quickly slurped down the soggy, green mass.

Its large ear twitched as Leaf softly whispered, "Thank you." Leaf dropped the willow stick and hurried to crouch in the cedar's roots with the others. The moose loped off good-naturedly along the edge of the lake searching for more sweet moss.

Immediately Star sprinted down the same trail they had followed to reach the lake. The stickytoes trotted behind her in a line. They lifted their sensitive bellies and tails up high above the rough, scratchy needles, and, with oddly bent legs, they scurried hastily after their beloved Star.

Leaf followed the stickytoes on the path through the dying trees. He felt uncomfortably warm. He glanced up and was startled to see the sun shining directly down at them. There were no green needles or fronds on the dead branches to block the sun's hot rays. Leaf blinked in the intense light. It was only midday yet Leaf felt like a whole season had passed since he left the Old Seeder this morning. Leaf blinked again and shielded his eyes to see better in the bright daylight. At once he stumbled over a brittle stick, and with an unnerving *snap,* it cracked in two.

Star glanced back at Leaf and frowned. She waved her hand ever so slightly reminding him to be completely silent.

At once, Leaf felt uneasy. The forest was so still and so creepy. As they jogged through the dying forest, he wondered if they were safe.

CHAPTER TWELVE

MOOK WAKES UP

Whisper snored gently in the scraggly whitebark pine tree. Her nose twitched as if tickled by dandelion fluff. Her tiny claws scratched the air as if she dug up cappynuts stored in the soft earth. She dreamed of the treats she had tucked away in the emerald forest.

Pappo sat beside Mook and piled more ice on Mook's legs, chest, and arms. Only Mook's barely-leafed head stuck out of the twinkly sparkles of ice. It was fortunate that Twigs are able to endure extreme cold and intense heat. A Twig could live if stuck in ice, but not the brittlebark. All traces of brittlebark die if frozen. Even then, Pappo knew Mook would only get well if he wasn't already too fragile. Otherwise he might simply fade away into his dreams forever. Pappo could not yet tell which might happen.

Mook moaned. "Star! Star!"

Pappo patted the snow pack, worried. *If only I knew what bothered him.*

Suddenly Mook's fingers stirred under the ice and broke free. Then he bolted upright and with frenzied movements tried to push away the ice pack. "I must get to Star and Moon!" he cried.

Firmly, Pappo pushed Mook's shoulders down to keep him from clawing his way out of the pack. "Easy, easy, old Twig." Pappo soothed him. "You are very sick and packed in ice. I brought you here to the Long Ice to get well."

"Ice pack?" Mook looked around, confused. He wrung his hands together. His eyes had been glazed over but now, slowly, they cleared. Mook was finally free of the deadly brittlebark disease.

Patiently and gently, Pappo brushed the ice off the frail Twig. "I'm Needles of the Old Seeder Twigs," Pappo said. "Take it slow," he cautioned Mook. "Come now. Step out of the ice slowly. You may get dizzy if you move too fast." Pappo held Mook's arm and guided the old Twig to where Whisper sat in the tree.

Whisper was awake and squinted anxiously at Mook. Pappo could see by her expression she didn't want to carry the old Twig on her back again. She scampered off and pretended to search for seeds in the loose rocks.

Mook sat down and leaned against the ancient twisted whitebark tree. Pappo offered him water from a cappynut shell. "How do you feel now?" he asked. "Try curling your toes!"

Mook sipped the water. He gazed in wonder at the vast mountain of ice and snow surrounding them. He stretched his fingers and toes. Then abruptly he covered his face with his hands and said, "Have I failed?" His voice was full of sorrow. "Are they all lost?"

Pappo shook his head and said, "I'm sorry, but I don't know what you're talking about. You've been dream talking since Pesky brought you here to our forest. All we know is you were very ill and that you came from the North Forest."

"Oh, no!" Mook was stunned. "Hasn't anyone gone to help the babes? How long have I been packed in ice?" He tried to stand, but his skinny, brown legs shook terribly. The effort defeated him and he plopped back into the roots of the old tree.

"Now, now! Rest, first! Don't worry," Pappo said. "You have to get well. You've only been in the ice for about a day. Not so long at all. Who's in trouble? Where are they? You kept talking about a star and a moon and biters. And are there babes somewhere left alone? Is Star your haven? Please, tell me everything and we'll help you!"

Mook held his head in his hands for a while. Finally he lifted his sad eyes and gazed into Pappo's. "The bark-biters came to our pretty forest. They eat trees from the inside out. At first, there were only a few, but then more and more came. Before long, they began to attack Twigs.

"Only a few creatures, like spiders and stickytoes will eat barkbiters. Eagles and hawks will feast on them, too, but even then there were not enough hunters in the forest to drive them away. The biters have sharp pinchers that pierce through the toughest tree bark. They can't fly, but they can crawl up trees and jump on you. They can't swim either, but if we tried to escape by water, eagles snatched us up for their nests, and the fish sucked us up like lake flies. Our beautiful forest slowly died around us.

"It was then that all of the forest branches of the North Twigs decided they must destroy the barkbiters.

They gathered their fiercest weapons to attack the evil creatures and drive them from the North Forest.

"But it was already too late. Hundreds of biters overwhelmed them. Only a few of the North Twigs survived. I led my dear Star and Moon, and six tiny babes to a cave to hide. It's only a matter of time before the barkbiters discover it. Star's friends, the stickytoes and looksalot, are their guards and bring them food and water every day. But it's only a matter of time now," Mook repeated. His head drooped and his gnarled hands shook.

Pappo didn't know what to say. He had never heard of barkbiters or stickytoes. He remembered what a looksalot was from old Twig tales. He was still unsure who Star and Moon were. He did understand though, whoever they were, they certainly needed help. It also sounded like it might be very dangerous to rescue them.

Pappo scratched his chin. Then he had an idea. Perhaps the Cappynut Twigs might help. He was still considering this when Mook finally raised his eyes once more to stare into Pappo's.

"Perhaps it's not too late. Maybe there's a chance?" Mook asked, looking hopeful. At once he urged Pappo, "We must go to the North Forest at once. We must go now!" He stopped speaking abruptly, suddenly confused, and said, "But I don't know the way back."

"You don't know the way?" Pappo asked, alarmed. "How did you find us?"

"Pesky must have seen you when he flew over your forest. I only remember taking off from the cave and when we landed. I must have fainted or slept the whole way." Mook searched around as if Pesky were hiding in the rocks. "Where *is* Pesky?"

"He's at my haven, the Old Seeder. He seemed quite happy to eat the worms there and wait with my son Leaf," Pappo assured him. "Now, don't worry anymore, Mook. We'll rescue all the Twig babes and Star and Moon. We need to get some food into you first! Do you think you could ride Whisper?" Pappo motioned to the chipmunk.

Mook looked skeptically at Whisper, who now stood nearer the old Twig with a curious expression on her face. Tufts of dried grass hung forgotten from her mouth. "Did I ride her up here?" he wondered aloud.

"She'll take good care of you." Pappo laughed at Mook's expression. Pappo motioned for Whisper to come closer.

LEAF & THE SKY OF FIRE

The speckled chipmunk gently stepped near Mook and patiently waited for the old Twig to grip the braid around her neck. Her eyes were warm and forgiving. She seemed to be thinking, *well, maybe he's not so crazy after all.* She pushed her tiny wet nose into Mook's ear to encourage him along.

Mook chuckled and waved away her nose. "Whisper, huh?" Mook appeared less anxious about riding her. Before he climbed onto her shoulders, Mook turned to Pappo and said seriously, "Needles, I don't have the words to thank you. For my life. For helping with this rescue. I can only warn you that it will be very dangerous, and if you choose not to go back with me, I understand."

"Just get well!" Pappo exclaimed. "I'm not sure how we'll find your cave though. The North Forest is immense and a Twig is easily lost there. But we'll try."

"Don't worry about that!" Mook spoke confidently. "Pesky is amazing! He can find his way anywhere just as if he were guided by the brightest star in the night sky! He'll lead us right to the cave!"

"Great!" Pappo answered.

Pappo boosted Mook's weak body onto Whisper. "We'll leave for the North Forest as soon as we return to the Old Seeder. I suppose Whisper could stand another adventure, eh?" He winked at Whisper, who blinked her curly eyelashes sweetly.

She didn't understand Pappo's words, but she nodded her head anyway. She trotted off cheerfully, bouncing Mook on her shoulders.

"Whoa, now!" Pappo cautioned Whisper. "Let's take it a little slower there."

Pappo took Whisper's braided leash, checked to be sure Mook was settled, and led her carefully down the trail, through the loose rocks, and into the gulch which led to the green forest. Mook's head nodded to the rhythm of Whisper's delicate steps.

"Just wait until you meet my son Leaf." Pappo chatted happily over his shoulder to his sleepy companion. "He's a clever and brave young Twig. He'll be a great help to us on our journey north."

CHAPTER THIRTEEN

THE BARKBITER BATTLE

Leaf, Star, Click, Chirp, and Crunch silently sprinted through the dying forest. The stickytoes sucked in their orange bellies and scuttled along the trail. Even their tails were held up high in a rigid curve behind them. Leaf realized they were trying very hard to keep from making any noise at all.

Star trotted quickly, without even a flutter of dust to mark her movement. Leaf tried to keep pace with the four in front of him but it was difficult to hurry and watch the unfamiliar path at the same time. Leaf stumbled and tripped over an empty, brittle, seed pod, and he muttered under his breath. Star glanced over her shoulder and glowered at him. Leaf frowned back.

As they ran along, Leaf wondered about these barkbiters. Obviously they were very dangerous. *But how could bugs—barkbiters—destroy an entire forest?* He glanced at the dying trees. *Why couldn't the Twigs here stop them? It's all just too unbelievable!* Still, he knew he must guide Star and the Twig babes to the log bridge as quickly as possible just in case what Star told him was true.

It was then that Leaf heard soft scurries like dozens of scratchy legs in the pine needles around them. He glimpsed shadows flickering just beyond their narrow trail. The shadows kept pace with them. Alarmed, Leaf ran past the prancing stickytoes, up to Star, and tugged at her arm. She never slowed but only glanced knowingly at him, and nodded grimly. *She already knows,* Leaf realized. *It was the barkbiters!*

"Star," he whispered as quietly as possible, "they'll follow us back to the cave!"

"I know," she answered sharply, her voice tense and low. "Didn't you notice that we've been running in circles? I don't know what else to do. We must lose them somehow. There are too many for my stickytoes to fight off!"

Leaf peered into the shadows. He wondered how many barkbiters were following them. *Well,* he thought, *one thing is for sure. There will be more and more gathering, and we can't wait for that!* "Star," Leaf whispered again, "I'll set them on fire with my stone!"

"Oh, right," she answered sarcastically. "You might get one or two!

Irritated with her rudeness, Leaf stopped abruptly and yanked Star's arm to make her stop, too. At the same moment, he swiftly pulled his saver from his shoulder strap's back loop.

The creepy, scratching noises stopped instantly. The wavering shadows froze.

The stickytoes became alarmed and confused. They rushed up to Star and curled around her legs.

"Watch," Leaf said loudly and fearlessly. He jabbed the saver into the earth and carefully rolled the stick between his flat hands until it caught the sun. Immediately a powerful beam burst from the stone and burned into the bark of a nearby tree. The bark smoldered at once. A wisp of smoke floated in the air. Swiftly, Leaf spun the beam in a circle around them.

Leaf and Star heard frantic scratches erupt in the dry needles then the sounds of the barkbiters scurried away into the forest.

"See?" Leaf grinned triumphantly at Star. She only pointed up, silent and grim.

Leaf looked up. Pudgy, black bodies floated awkwardly down from the limbs of pine trees on stubby, dark wings. Thorny legs clawed the air furiously. Curved pinchers clacked and dripped slime. Worst of all, the barkbiters' glowing, ruby eyes stared only at Leaf.

Leaf screamed—shocked. Instinctively he crouched down and ducked behind Star.

Star punched him in the arm to bring him to his senses. She grabbed Leaf's strap and yanked him to his feet beside her.

The stickytoes' mouths opened to a wide grin. They curled their long, pink tongues in anticipation.

Leaf's hands trembled but quickly he gripped his saver and swung it in a slow circle above their heads. Star and the stickytoes crouched down and pressed around Leaf's legs. He swung the long walking stick faster and faster until it became a shiny, flat, humming shield!

Like stones skipping over water, barkbiters bounced off the disc and slammed into the trunks of nearby trees. They lay crumpled, smashed in the roots. Their green blood dribbled from split bellies.

But more barkbiters kept floating down from the trees—their glowing red eyes fixed on Leaf.

"Star," Leaf cried out frantically, "can you swing the saver?"

"Yes, of course," she shouted back. She grabbed the saver from Leaf's hands, swung with all her strength, and kept the saver-shield whirring and blurry above them.

Leaf tugged his whistletube from his strap pocket, lifted it to his lips, and blew hard. But instead of a pretty melody, a horrible screech filled the air. Star and the stickytoes flinched at the gruesome sound. Leaf blew the harsh, screeching blast over and over, non-stop. It sounded like a wounded creature screaming in pain.

Soon an enormous shadow swept across them, soared away then flew back. The shadow spiraled down closer and closer, in tighter circle. Piercing black eyes investigated the scene below. It was a fearsome hunter from the sky—an eagle. Curious, it watched the bizarre sight of barkbiters slamming into trees, and studied the spinning, humming disc. For eagles, wounded creatures in the forest are an easy meal.

The barkbiters cowered beneath the huge shadow of the eagle. Threatened from above, they scattered into the forest.

It became very quiet except for the humming of the saver, which Star still whirled. She stopped at last, gasping, and leaned on the strong stick. Leaf stood up and waved furiously at the eagle to be sure it understood they were not the dying prey it sought. With a tip of its powerful wing, it flew away.

"Leaf," Star breathed in relief, "you did it!"

"We both did!" he answered then looked around warily. Immediately he said, "Uh, can we go now?"

"Yes, hurry!" Star answered. She gripped the saver and raced off down the trail.

The stickytoes sprinted after her without a backward glance, their tails curled high above their backs. Leaf hesitated and glanced around. He felt as if he had forgotten something important. A thin wisp of smoke curled in the air, but Leaf did not notice it. He shrugged and shook his head, puzzled at the feeling, then bolted after Star.

Star, Leaf, and the stickytoes reached the cave at last and slid through the mass of spider webs. They fell onto the red clay floor, gasping for breath.

Veil closed the webs behind them with his flat nose. He rolled his eyes in two directions so he could watch the cave's entrance and Star at the same time. The stickytoes licked their scratches and blinked at Veil with warm, shiny eyes.

With wide eyes, the Twig babes sat very still, pressed against the granite rock. They tried to blend in with the cave wall as they had been taught to do whenever some unexpected movement or noise frightened them.

"Did they follow us?" worried Leaf.

Moon peered through the webs. "Barkbiters?" he asked. "No, I don't see anything. Veil, do you?" The looksalot swung his scaly head back and forth. "I think we're safe," Moon reassured everyone. "What happened? Did the barkbiters attack?"

"Yes," Star answered, still breathing heavily. "But we fought them off! That was quick thinking, Leaf!" She laughed.

Leaf still trembled as he lay sprawled out on the cool clay.

Star looked at Moon with silver, shining eyes. "You should have seen it, Moon! First Leaf burned the barkbiters back with a circle of smoke. Then he swung his saver over our heads and the barkbiters bounced off it and were smashed into trees! Then Leaf blew his whistle and it sounded like some poor creature screaming in the forest so an eagle flew over. All the barkbiters ran away!"

Moon stared at her in disbelief.

Star added seriously, "For a moment there, though, I thought they had us." Then she grinned brightly at Leaf.

"Me too," Leaf nodded. He sat up and grinned back at Star. "You were great!"

Astonished, Moon looked from Star to Leaf, then back to Star. He shook his head hopelessly. They had just escaped barkbiters, yet Star and Leaf were grinning like two foolish stickytoes.

We're going to be very lucky to escape this forest, thought Moon. *These two nutheads act like it's a great adventure to fight barkbiters!*

CHAPTER FOURTEEN

ESCAPE

"Moon, you must leave right away," Leaf urged the young Twig. "My Pappo must be warned about the barkbiters before he comes to look for me. Can you call Pesky now?"

"Of course," Moon sounded irritated. "But first I have to tie on the carry-cradles to the stickytoes."

"We can do it," Star reassured him. "Leaf's right. There's no time to waste. You must hurry. Call Pesky."

Moon moved toward the webs. "Wait!" Leaf cried out. "Be sure to watch Pesky's path. You will have to lead Pappo to the great log that bridges the chasm. It's the only way across to my forest. Pesky knows where it is. He'll show you."

Moon looked doubtful. "Won't PapaMook know where to go?"

Leaf paused a moment to consider his words then sympathetically said, "Moon, he was very ill when Pesky brought him to us. There's no way to know if he's still dream talking or not, or even if he knows where he is at all. There's only one thing for sure. My Pappo will come looking for me."

Star and Moon glanced at each other. With a questioning look, they both frowned at Leaf.

"Well, you see, I didn't exactly tell him I was coming," Leaf explained, sheepishly. "He might be a little upset."

"Well, just great!" Moon blurted out. "So now I'm supposed to bring your Pappo to some big log that crosses a gorge and only Pesky is supposed to know where it is! And your Pappo's mad at you, too! I'm going to be lucky enough to not get thrown off Pesky, much less find your Pappo, or this giant gorge log bridge!" he said, exasperated.

Star interrupted his tirade, "Moon, you can do this! Now, do you have water and food with you?" She inspected the pockets on his shoulder strap and checked to be sure his cappynut shell was full of water.

Moon pushed her hands away, grim and unhappy. "I'm all set except for Pesky." He frowned at Leaf. "I hope that nuthead tooler won't toss me into the cliffs. He's never let me ride him before! I don't know why he will now!"

Leaf looked surprised. "Oh, all you have to do is give him some treats. Just toss him a couple of berries, grab his braid, and hop on!"

Moon obviously did not believe Leaf.

"Really, it's great fun! Give him some berries! He'll do anything for berries!" Leaf encouraged Moon. "Just remember to hang on tight and don't pull out his feathers!"

Moon stared at Leaf for a moment then a slight smile played on his lips. "Well, at least I get to get out of this cave, anyway!" He paused and grew serious. "Leaf, I meant to thank you for coming. Please take good care of Star and the Twig babes. I'll see you soon."

"Fare well," nodded Leaf, not knowing what else to say.

Star took Moon by the elbow and led him through the spider webs. Leaf heard a low whistle and the beat of wings. *It must be Pesky*, he thought. After a short while, Star stepped back into the cave. Tiny, silver tears clung to her eyelashes.

"He's gone?" Leaf asked.

She nodded and sadly turned away.

"Is Moon gone? Is Moon gone?" the babes all chirped at once.

"Yes, sweeties," Star soothed them. "We're all going for a long trip now and you get to ride the stickytoes!"

The babes clapped, giggled gleefully, and rolled around on the clay, pulling at their toes.

Star admonished them at once. "But you must promise to be very, very quiet all the way or you can't go! We're going to sneak past the biters!"

Wide eyed, Moss, Breeze, Cone, Mist, and Sand shook their heads up and down vigorously with their tiny lips clamped shut just to show how quiet they could be. Stubbornly, Pool blew popping, noisy bubbles. Star looked at him sharply to be sure he understood that she was deadly serious. He looked away, avoided her angry gaze, but stopped popping bubbles, at once.

"Very good," Star whispered. "The trip starts now."

Star tied the cradles to each stickytoes and lifted the babes into the seats, two in each cradle—Breeze with Moss, Cone with Mist, and Sand with Pool. Star hoped Sand's good nature would stop Pool from mis-behaving. Click, Chirp, and Crunch spread their legs far apart and lay their flat bellies on the ground as Star secured the cradles to their bark shields. She fastened the babes' braided shoulder straps across their chests to hold them tight in their seats. Star laid bags stuffed with seeds and nuts over the shoulders of the stickytoes. They grinned widely at her in anticipation of treats later on. Star lifted a strap over her own shoulders which was loaded down with two cappynut shells full of water. The stickytoes swayed gently toward the cave's sunlit entrance.

Leaf eyed the sled that Moon put together to pull the looksalot. A long, forked stick lay by Veil. A braided rope had been threaded through a knothole at its tip and the ends lay on the clay floor. It was divided into two large loops. *These must be for my shoulders*, Leaf figured out. He stepped in front of the looksalot and tried to catch his eye. Unfortunately, his eyes continu-ally rolled in opposite directions. Finally one eye fixed on Leaf for a moment, so Leaf spoke to that eye directly.

"Uh, Veil," Leaf began. Veil's eye rolled away. Leaf continued anyway. "Veil, could you please stand on this stick?" Leaf stepped backward and politely made a wide, sweeping gesture inviting the looksalot to move onto the stick-sled.

Veil rocked back and forth, heavily nodded his scaly head, and slowly lifted a two-toed foot. Disturbingly, he held it there motionless.

Leaf looked aghast. *What was wrong?*

Star chuckled behind him. In a low, cool voice she spoke confidently. "Veil, on the stick, please!"

With his greenish-blue tail coiled into a tight spiral and held up off the floor, Veil stepped painfully slowly nearer the stick. He lifted one hand, along with a foot at the same time, until he finally climbed aboard. He balanced delicately on his stick-sled. For some strange, unknown reason Veil looked proud. The looksalot clutched the stick with his two-toed hands and two-toed feet, and happily rolled his eyes around in circles. He was ready to go.

"All right, then," Leaf said, not really sure what to do next.

"Here," Star helped him lift the loops over his shoulders. "I'll help you pull Veil out of the cave."

Motioning to the babes to be quiet, Star waved to the stickytoes, who waited in a line to follow. Then she grabbed hold of the braided rope behind Leaf's shoulders and pulled. Leaf tugged against the weight of the sled. He was surprised when the stick slid easily across the floor.

Star smiled at him as he swiftly pulled Veil through the webs from the cave to the bright sun beyond. *At least pulling Veil will be easy*, Leaf thought. *This sled was a good idea.*

Star helped tug Veil over a mound of rocks then pointed to a path in the woods which would take them uphill toward the rocky ridge.

As Leaf and Star stepped quietly along the path, he glanced over his shoulder. The stickytoes rocked from side to side as they stepped out of the dark cave. The babes rubbed their eyes in the bright sunlight and yawned. Leaf wondered if Click, Chirp, and Crunch were deliberately rocking the little ones to sleep already. He caught sight of Veil's huge, flat-mouthed grin, and he knew the looksalot was enjoying the ride. *He's probably glad to get out of that dark cave,* thought Leaf.

Leaf hesitated when Star paused on the side of the trail. "Everything all right?" asked Leaf, a little too loudly.

Star gently placed her hand on Leaf's arm. "I'm going to follow behind the stickytoes," she said softy, and glanced uneasily around. "I'll watch out for any danger. Do you know where to go?"

Leaf pointed up to the crest of the steep ridge. "Let's go up there. There are fewer trees and we can see farther," he said, hoping his strategy made sense and they would be safe. He added in a whisper, "In case they come after us."

Star nodded in agreement. She waited as the odd procession of stickytoes passed her on the trail. Click, Crunch, and Chirp marched silently past, grinning at nothing in particular. Star smiled reassuringly at the babes and watched their sleepy heads nod as they rocked in their carry cradles. Falling into step behind Chirp, she was last in line.

Leaf pulled Veil up the dusty path. It led toward a narrow, winding, steep trail which traversed the face of the sheer cliff. Huge slabs and boulders lay crushed at the base of the ridge. Having grown weak over time, the pieces of granite had broken away and crashed into rubble. Leaf looked up, worried. This clumsy looksalot will need to be very calm and still on this scary trek up the ridge or they might both tumble over the edge. Testing the weight and balance of the looksalot, Leaf tugged Veil's sled a little faster. It slid easily now, but he wondered if he would be strong enough to pull this silly creature all the way to the top.

Leaf stared up at the crest. *There's probably plenty of caves up there*, he thought. He studied the shadowy crevices on the steep cliffs. *We better find one before twilight. All we need is a cave.*

CHAPTER FIFTEEN

THE CAPPYNUT TWIGS

Pappo, Mook, and Whisper were embraced by the deep green of the forest as they finally left the gray rocks of the ridge behind. Loose gravel gave way to springy moss. Whisper's sore paws healed as they sunk into the moist grass on the trail. She walked quicker, anxious to find her juicy berries and plump seeds by the Old Seeder once more. Mook swayed in the carry-cradle and hung his head sleepily on Whisper's neck. Her fragrant fur lulled him into dreams. He slept peacefully for the first time in a long while.

Pappo led them back the long way by a sparkling stream and through a gully. They came to a dark green hollow near an enormous, ancient cappynut tree. Its limbs reached high above them, and spread into a tangled, twisted mass of branches which blocked the blue sky.

Slender shadows moved in the roots of the tree.

Pappo called out, "I've been keeping an eye out for you, Sapper! Is that Ruffle and Tuffle in those roots too?"

Mook jerked his head up suddenly, obviously alarmed.

"Come out, Cappynut Twigs!" Pappo urged. "Are you all there?"

Whisper and Mook watched in surprise as the shadows dissolved into three taller-than-average Twigs with noses as pointed as rose thorns. And their hair! It sprouted as if they wore a bouquet of tangled leaves. Their mischievous eyes peeked out from within and could barely be seen. They dressed in feathers which were bound around their waists and spread out behind their backs. The wispy feathers stuck straight up behind their leafy heads like upside-down bird tails. They wore green braids around their ankles. Wooden slingers—a sort of sling shot—were shoved into their grass belts. Sapper was the tallest. He was the paps of Ruffle and Tuffle—twin Twigs who, although similar in looks, dressed completely differently. Ruffle wore the feathers of a blue jay. Tuffle wore those from the belly of a yellow thrush. Sunbeams blinked through their fluffy, vibrant, outrageous outfits and the twin Twigs fairly glowed in the sun. They all grinned as if they had played a great trick on Pappo.

"I see you are still more birds than Twigs!" laughed Pappo. "And when will you give up those slingers and get some real hunting tools like a saver and a whistletube?"

At once Ruffle pulled a long feather from his belt and blew a sharp note into the hollow tube. The birds scattered noisily above them.

The other twin, Tuffle, pulled his slinger from his belt, and loaded a small pebble into its wide, flaxen band. He stuck out his tongue as he concentrated. He aimed the pebble at a high limb far above them. Tuffle let go of the band, and the pebble whizzed away, only a blur speeding straight at a single leaf. The pebble snapped the leaf from its skinny stem with a loud *thwack!* The leaf spiraled down softly down through the sunlit boughs and landed gently at Pappo's feet. Tuffle winked and grinned at his brother, Ruffle.

"I'll match our tools against your tools any day, Needles!" challenged Sapper. He clapped his hands in praise of his talented young sons.

Pappo and Sapper laughed joyfully, happy to be in one another's company. They clasped each other's shoulders in a cheery Twig greeting. Ruffle and Tuffle joined the friendly huddle, laughing with delight. Finally, they all disentangled themselves.

Tired of the long journey from Echo Peak, Whisper shook Mook from her back and hopped over to nibble clover and dandelion tips. She watched the merry Twigs out of the corner of her eye, and groomed her quivering whiskers until they shone silver.

Still very weak, Mook plopped down on the grass. In a tired voice, he said, "Allo, Cappynut Twigs. I'm Mook from the Land of Dancing Sky Lights."

"Oh, yes." Pappo suddenly remembered his manners. "Here is our new friend, Mook." Pappo swept his arm in Mook's direction and stepped over to help lift the frail Twig stand up on his shaky legs. "He's been terribly sick with brittlebark. I've just brought him back from the Long Ice."

"So he's had an ice pack, then, eh, Needles?" Sapper asked keenly.

"Yes. He's still weak but all well now," Pappo answered although he was obviously still worried about the old Twig.

"So did you need our help to carry him?" Sapper wondered, looking in the direction of Whisper and her carry-cradle.

Ruffle and Tuffle ignored Mook. They were fascinated with Whisper. They watched her fastidious grooming ritual with great interest. Tentatively, Ruffle reached out and touched her tiny black nose. She sneezed and turned her back to continue grooming without interruption.

"No, it's not that exactly." Pappo hesitated, unsure how to ask for help.

Sapper stood with hands on his hips and scrutinized the elderly Twig. Pappo kept lifting Mook up and leaning him against a tree trunk but the old Twig kept sliding down onto the moss.

Mook shook his head as if to clear spider webs from his thoughts. He rubbed the thin, white leaves on his head. Finally, he waved Pappo's help away and just sat slumped over in the soft, deep moss.

Pappo shrugged and with a serious expression turned to face the Cappynut Twigs. He decided to ask for help in the most formal, respectful manner he could muster. He began, "Sapper. Ruffle. Tuffle. This is Mook of the North. He flew here on his tooler, Pesky, to ask for help. There are Twig babes and two other young Twigs stranded in a cave very far away in the North Forest. Mook has come seeking help to rescue them."

Without any hesitation, Sapper, Ruffle, and Tuffle turned to Mook. All of them spoke up at once. "Of course we'll help, old Twig! We'll come at once. Shall we leave now? Let's go!"

Pappo held up his hands and patted the air, trying to calm them down. "Thank you, thank you, dear Cappynut friends, but there is something more."

The Cappynut Twigs looked at him curiously.

Pappo paused, his eyes huge with foreboding. Ominously, he warned them. "There is great danger in the North Forest."

Sapper, Ruffle, and Tuffle stood quietly for just a moment, then immediately shouted eagerly. "Great! We laugh at danger! We grin at it too! We're in!"

"Wait! Wait!" Pappo waved his hands at them and tried once again to calm their enthusiasm. "You need to know that there are barkbiters there—huge, vicious bugs that might attack us at anytime. They destroyed Mook's forest and nearly all of the North Twigs. Please know that this rescue will be very dangerous!" Pappo paused. "I will understand if you decide to not come," he added.

The Cappynut Twigs stood silent, scratched their chins and studied the branches above them thoughtfully. Sapper glanced at his sons but they only nodded back. So at last, Sapper declared, "It doesn't matter! We're Twigs! We stick together!"

Ruffle and Tuffle stepped politely over to Mook and bowed. They spoke in unison. "Don't worry anymore, old Twig. We'll help."

Mook let out a long breath and cried, "I have no words to thank you! But we must leave right away. The babes are trapped in the cave!"

"Now, now," Pappo soothed him. "We'll leave soon enough." He turned to Whisper. "Come here, sweet Whisper." As he re-fastened the carry-cradle securely on her speckled back he continued, "First, we must go to the Old Seeder for something to eat and drink. Ruffle and Tuffle, you remember Leaf's Mumma, Ivy? She still makes the best sapsuckers in the forest and she'll want to prepare some food for the journey, too." Carefully, Pappo lifted Mook onto Whisper's shoulders. Mook stroked the gentle chipmunk's fuzzy, tufted ears, grateful for her help.

"So do you think Ivy made some of her delicious berry mashcakes?" Sapper asked hopefully. Ruffle and Tuffle stared pointedly at Pappo. Their eyes gleamed with expectation.

"Surely, surely," Pappo reassured them. "And mint tea too!"

They walked slowly along a deer trail, mindful of the frail Twig clinging to the golden braid around Whisper's neck.

Sapper and Pappo spoke about their adventures long ago when they were young. The twins hid furtively in the shadows alongside them and practiced being invisible— as young Twigs should do. However, their curiosity to hear the older Twigs' stories occasionally caused them to trip and fall into the path, spoiling their attempts to hide.

Sapper and Pappo laughed at the two young Twigs, and proudly compared Leaf, Ruffle, and Tuffle's skills as paps often do.

Before long, the small group reached the Old Seeder. Ivy had been watching for Pappo from the haven's knothole. As they reached the tangled roots below, she poked her head out.

"Allo! Welcome!" Mumma called out. Fern peeked down. Buddy and Burba pushed around Fern to stare at the strange-looking company in the roots of their tree home.

Pappo looked up and, even from far below, noticed the worry on Mumma's face. Something was wrong. At once alarmed, he searched the limbs and quickly noticed that Pesky was not tied to the branch outside their knothole. And Leaf. *Where was Leaf?* It took him only an instant to realize where Leaf had gone. Pappo caught his breath. *Leaf has taken Pesky to the North Forest! But he does not know about the barkbiters!*

Pappo's eyes met Mumma's but he hid his concern for Leaf from her. Carefully he assisted Mook up the rough bark of the Old Seeder. He considered what he should do. They needed Pesky to guide them north. How would they find the babes now?

Mumma welcomed them all into the knothole. She and Fern bustled around finding soft moss and ferns so their visitors might sit comfortably. A clear stone hung in a knothole and caught an evening's last ray of sun. It warmed the mint tea perfectly. Pappo spoke quietly to Mumma as she filled up her blue-spotted robin egg-shells with the fragrant tea. He stated flatly, "Leaf has gone north."

"Yes," Mumma nodded with her voice low. "Now, now, Needles, I thought he should go, too. He just wanted to help find the Twig babes—if they're even there."

Pappo's mouth tightened.

Mumma continued, "Now, Needles, I understand how he felt," she urged Pappo to understand, too. "He didn't know when you and Mook might return." She glanced at Pappo's grim face again. "Needles, he promised to return right away." She smiled brightly.

Pappo stared at the misty tea, not knowing how to tell Mumma about the barkbiters.

All at once, Mumma realized Pappo wasn't only grim, he was afraid. Immediately she became alarmed. With wide, worried eyes, she asked fearfully, "What is it?"

"Ivy, Ivy!" Sapper called out to the two huddled over the eggshells. "Your berry mashcakes are as delicious as ever! And this seedpod bread is excellent! Is there more mint tea ready?"

"Yes, yes, of course, dear Sapper," Mumma answered absentmindedly as she reluctantly broke away from Pappo. The guests must be served. "Yes, please have more tea. There is plenty."

Pappo stepped into the middle of the Twigs which now were sitting in a cozy circle on the floor. He held up his hands as if giving a speech. "Friends, I have some news. My son Leaf has left on Pesky. He has flown to the North Forest to rescue the stranded Twigs by himself."

Mook looked shocked. "How will we find our way there?" he cried out at once. His eyes were wide. Alarmed, he turned his head from one Twig to the other as if they had an answer.

There was an awkward, silent pause.

Sensing trouble, Fern ushered Buddy and Burba into their own sleeping hollow, away from the older Twigs. She dropped a worn, red leaf over the entry behind her and followed after them. Quickly, Mumma stuck three sweet sapsuckers into Fern's hand as she left to watch over the babes.

Mumma knew something was terribly wrong, but didn't know what. Clearly, there was some danger in the North Forest that neither she nor Leaf had guessed was there. She now realized it had been dangerous to let him go alone. Mumma stood, tense and silent, with her back pressed against the warm, smooth wood of the hollow tree trunk. She wrung her hands over and over. Her eyes glimmered with tears.

"I can take us to the gorge!" Sapper said firmly. "I know the way there."

"Good," Pappo said slowly. "But how will we get across?"

They all sat silent, thinking about this new problem. The Twigs knew the gorge defined the north border of their world. No way had been found to cross over. So no one had any ideas.

Mook dropped his head into his hands. He knew there was no longer any hope of rescuing the babes. Concerned for the sad, old Twig, Mumma took his hand and led him into Leaf's small sleeping hollow. Weary and troubled, he crumpled at once onto Leaf's moss bed and fell asleep.

Mumma returned right away. Her hands trembled. *Was Leaf trapped in the North Forest without help? What was this horrible danger there?*

Steam from the simmering tea hovered around the anxious faces of the Twigs. The water bubbled, forgotten. The Twigs sat deep in thought. They refused to believe the great chasm was impassable but no one had a plan.

All of a sudden, a noisy, flapping crash rattled the haven's round door. Alarmed, the Twigs stared at its small window, afraid to move. A white, leafy head flashed in the dark outside, and the next moment a young Twig with pale gray, penetrating eyes stepped through the knothole. He put his hands on his hips and stood arrogantly before them. Scornfully, he scrutinized the older Twigs who were crowded together on the floor of the misty haven.

Without any introduction, Moon asked irritably, "Is there a Pappo here?"

CHAPTER SIXTEEN

SHADOW IN THE FOREST

Star stumbled on the steep, narrow, rocky trail. She was very tired. A glowing, red sun sank behind her. It slipped reluctantly behind the bare tree tips as if sad it must leave the Twigs who still struggled toward the crest. Star blinked the dust from her eyes and, too weary to lift her silver-leafed head, simply followed the sweeping marks left on the path by the stickytoes' tails.

Leaf heard pebbles fall over the edge of the high trail. He looked over his shoulder. He was worried about Star. Her slender, young Twig frame appeared as a wispy silhouette against the rose-colored strips of clouds. Star stumbled again. Leaf could do little except continue up the ridge.

Wide bands of light danced in the darkening sky. The bands had many colors, and moved as if they were giant waves rolling upon a dark blue shore. As Leaf pulled Veil up the narrow trail along the cliff face, he watched the wavy bands in awe until he slipped on some loose rocks, too. Quickly he steadied Veil who clutched the stick-sled and rolled his eyes in alarm. Cautiously, Leaf regained his footing. Veil eyed the deep ravine below nervously and clung to the stick even tighter. Leaf murmured some soothing words to the worried looksalot then turned his attention once more to the winding, uphill path. But before long his eyes were drawn skyward once more to the incredible dancing lights.

Higher on the trail there were many shadowy crevices which cut into the granite wall. Leaf knew he must search the cliff and find shelter for the night, yet he could not tear his eyes from the sky's amazing radiance. Never before had he imagined a Land of Dancing Sky Lights even existed. The silky shades of blue, green, violet, and red rippled in the heavens playfully. They seemed so close. They beckoned to Leaf to touch them. Leaf lifted his hand then paused, embarrassed.

The trail widened to a ledge. Granite slabs leaned against the cliff, not yet totally dislodged. Leaf whispered over his shoulder to Star who trudged slowly behind the stickytoes, "We should rest here."

"Sure." Star sounded exhausted, although not as much from the trek, as from worry over the babes. The tiny babes rode the stickytoes quietly. Still, babes were babes and they made hand shadows on the path for fun. Their fingers formed odd creatures and they grinned at each other silently, stifling their giggles.

Leaf studied the deep cracks in the cliff. There were no caves but these three slabs before him formed a sort of lean-to, a shelter. Leaf could see a roomy, sandy floor through a crack in one of the slabs. There was no roof, but the walls of the granite tent were steep and smooth. Barkbiters would not easily scratch up these rocks. Leaf decided it was the safest place to spend the night.

In any case, Veil could stand guard. Veil had dozed often during his ride on the stick sled, so he should be able to stay awake. Leaf felt reassured. He halted their march, gratefully shrugged off the rope's loops, turned, bowed, and swept his arm in a wide motion inviting Veil to step off the stick.

Veil rocked back and forth, and finally moved completely off the sled with staggered, halting steps. His

eyes rolled in opposite directions. One fixed suspiciously on the shelter, the other looked for Star.

Gently, Leaf lifted the babes one by one from their
cradles and pushed them through the cleft in the slab.
The stickytoes easily slipped in. Veil, who was larger
than the stickytoes, had to squeeze himself through to
fit. He stretched his body until it was nearly flat, then
slowly and stubbornly pushed until he popped onto the
sand inside.

Leaf and Star paused outside for a moment. The
dying trees below faded into orange, ghostly skeletons
as the sun crept even lower behind them. The stars
blinked as Leaf and Star slipped into the small shelter.
Veil plodded over and squatted comfortably in front of
the narrow opening. The night guard was on duty.

Star pulled seeds and nuts from the stickytoes'
pouches as Leaf shared the water they carried in cappynut shells with the babes, Click, Crunch, Chirp, and
Veil. Star and Leaf waited until all of the others had
eaten then they finally ate too.

Sand, Moss, Breeze, Cone, and Mist drew pictures in
the sand for a while. Pool kicked sand at them. After a
while, they grew restless.

"Tell us a story," they pleaded.

Star simply shook her head and held her finger to her lips to quiet their cries. She dared not make any noise. In the clear night air, their voices would carry far and echo off the cliff.

Leaf sighed and worried. *Poor little Twig babes. This journey is so difficult for them.* Then he smiled. He had an idea. From within their rock shelter, they could easily see the glimmering sky lights dance. Leaf knelt, drew his saver from its strap loop, and stuck the walking stick in the sand of the rock shelter.

Puzzled, Star looked at him questioningly.

Leaf only grinned back. With the saver's stone, Leaf caught the bright gleams of the night lights.

They flashed a rainbow of colors which slid across the granite walls as if dancing wildly. The vibrant beams burst and sparkled above the awestruck Twigs. Not content to remain within the rock slabs, they sought the sky, soaring from the shelter, up the cliff face, and flying away to disappear and mix with the bands of light which filled the velvety sky.

"Oooh," the babes cooed in a whisper.

Star smiled. Leaf grinned. For a long time, he twisted the stone and flashed the colorful beams in the shelter until the babes finally lay their sleepy heads down on the sand and fell into playful dreams.

Below in the forest, a dark shadow wandered among the dying trees. The awesome beast was seeking food. It was far from any place familiar. Disturbed, it paced back and forth uneasily, shook its massive head, and stared up at the unusual sky lights— not the lights which danced in the night sky but the lights which flashed from the cliff.

The earth trembled with its tremendous weight, and the night creatures fled from its fearsome, warning growl. Restlessly, it lumbered up the narrow, steep path toward the vibrant lights dancing wildly from the granite rocks.

CHAPTER SEVENTEEN

STICKYTOES ON GUARD

In the very early dawn the stickytoes woke and nudged Veil aside. Now it was their turn to be on guard. Veil slowly made his way over to the babes, squeezed his eyes shut, and curled his long tail into a tight swirl. His skin changed color to the same tan as the sand. He fell asleep. Crunch, Click, and Chirp lay flat on their orange bellies and stared through the granite cracks at the fading night stars.

Before long, the sunrise spilled over the cliff. Glowing, pink waves fell down the rock walls and splashed over the rocks where the Twigs lay sleeping. The stickytoes patiently waited for tiny bugs to creep into the shelter, then took turns unfurling their stretchy tongues to smack them. They whacked, snatched, and crunched them until Star and Leaf stirred at the noise and sat up, still very sleepy.

The Twigs rubbed the sand from their eyes. Breeze rolled over, threw her arm across Pool, and her leg over Moss. The Twig babes snored gently. Cone, Mist, and Sand blinked and sat up right away, eager for the day's adventure. They tugged at the moss bags in search of seeds.

Star knelt beside Breeze, Moss, and Pool and gently shook them awake. She handed each babe some nuts or seeds and water in cappynut shells. Pool shoved his seeds in his mouth at once and then rolled pebbles at the other babes. Mist poured her water in the sand and patted it into odd shapes. Breeze, Moss, Cone, and Sand poured their water in the sand too. So Pool threw pebbles at their sand shapes which made the others turn away from the disagreeable Twig babe. Scowling at the backs of their heads, Pool took a big drink of water and spit it at Sand. She took a handful of sand and threw it at Pool.

Breeze yelled, "Pool's spitting water! Sand's throwing dirt 'cause Pool's spitting water!"

Exasperated, Star took Pool's arm and sat him in a small hollow by the slab wall. Then she took Sand to the other side of the shelter to sit by herself. She glanced back at Pool and saw him stick out his tongue at Breeze for tattling. Breeze began to cry.

"Pool!" Star admonished him, "behave!"

"I was just pretending to be Veil," he whined.

Star frowned at him then comforted Breeze with a gentle hug. "Please remember to be quiet," she reminded all of them with an urgent whisper. They fell silent at once. Star sighed and dug deeper into the moss bags. She found some tiny sugary balls of sap for each babe.

At last, Star rested beside Leaf. They sat with their backs turned away from the babes. Wearily, they gazed past the stickytoes to the dry, brittle trees below. Worry already clouded their young faces.

"We need to go soon," Leaf said. "Do you think Veil is rested enough?"

Star crawled over to the sleeping looksalot and laid her cheek against his scaly neck. Veil woke at her touch. Whispering softly, Star patted his nose. Veil rolled his eyes in a wide circle then nodded.

"He's fine," Star said softly to Leaf. "But the sticky-toes must have their skin dampened before they go back in the sun." She dumped the last of their water on the moss pack she held. "We're going to need more water," she said, tiredly. "The babes poured most of it in the sand."

The babes looked at her with guilty faces, and she couldn't help but frown at them. Quickly they pushed dry sand over the wet sand to hide it.

"Oh, never mind. It's all right," Star whispered. "Don't worry. We'll find more water." They smiled brightly at her.

"I'll find water," Leaf volunteered. "I'm sure there's water nearby." He stepped out on the ledge. "Listen! I hear splashing." He peered over the edge of the trail. "Look, Star, there's a little waterfall down there." Leaf pointed to a thin stream of water tumbling from a crevice below where they stood. It dropped straight down the sheer cliff wall.

Star peeked over the edge and looked worried. "It's so steep."

Leaf simply shrugged. "It doesn't look so hard." He ducked back in the shelter and laid his saver on the sand by Veil. He could climb down the rocks more quickly if he didn't have to worry about it. The water would be heavy enough in the cappynut shells to carry back up the cliff.

Star nodded reluctantly, "All right, then. But please be very careful."

Leaf hooked all of the cappynut shells on his strap's thorns then crawled backwards down the cliff. He braced his legs once when he slipped, but steadily he made his way down the rock wall to the waterfall. As soon as he reached it, he glanced up and waved to reassure Star.

Chirp squatted on the ledge and curiously watched Leaf hang onto the rock face below. Leaf shoved the cappynut shells under the meager trickle of water and quickly filled them up. He hooked the shells back onto his strap, and began to climb back up the cliff.

Suddenly, Leaf heard a shrill *chirp! chirp! chirp!* It was the urgent warning whistles of the stickytoes! A piercing *screech!* followed.

Leaf frantically pulled himself up the rock wall. Desperately, he grabbed at the crumbling granite and searched for a foothold. Finally he reached the flat ledge. Leaf was horrified!

Click, Chirp, and Crunch were crouched before the shelter's opening. They had created a barricade between a scary, snarling weasel with razor-sharp teeth and Veil, Star, and the Twig babes. The brave stickytoes hissed with half-opened mouths and pumped themselves up and down in a courageous display of ferocity. They puffed out their orange bellies and stared defiantly at the weasel.

The weasel crept just out of reach of the freakish-looking stickytoes. Its tail twitched impatiently and slapped the ground as it searched for a way to reach the sweet smell within the shelter. The weasel's body was so flexible it almost curled in two as it angrily paced back and forth.

Click, Crunch, and Chirp's were so swollen up, they looked twice their size. The weasel wanted nothing to do with the stickytoes, but it would not give up the hunt for the babes. It could smell the sweet, sugary sap in the shelter, and keenly watched the flickering shadows through the cleft in the granite slabs.

Frightened, Leaf had no idea how to help. With a sick feeling, he remembered he had left his saver in the shelter. *He had no weapon!* Just then Leaf felt the stones beneath his hands. At once, he threw a rock at the weasel, and another and another. The evil hunter swung its head around and spat at Leaf, warning him to stop. Leaf was off balance and couldn't hit him anyway. The weasel growled and bared his teeth but did not move from the sweet prey it stalked. Desperately, Leaf chucked another rock but it only skidded across the ledge and bounced off the cliff wall.

The stickytoes continuously pumped themselves up and down. The weasel paused. It seemed to be deciding which annoying creature to attack first . . . the weird-looking stickytoes or the helpless Twig whose aim was so pitiful?

Then a piece of granite whizzed out of the cave over the heads of the stickytoes. Then another and another flew out. The babes and Star threw shards of granite from the shelter as fast as they could break them off the slabs. The rocks zipped past the weasel's head, but it easily dodged them and none hit their mark. Awkwardly, Leaf tried to throw rocks with both hands at once until he nearly fell. The weasel dodged the rain of rocks easily. It simply chattered at them all with hateful, slicing sounds made through its teeth.

With a sudden unexpected rush the weasel sprang through the air at the stickytoes!

Instantly, Click and Chirp cast out their long tongues. Click's tongue wrapped around the weasel's tail just as Chirp's seized its skinny neck. The stickytoes tugged the weasel in opposite directions and stretched the weasel out between them. Crunch unfurled his tongue and swiftly wrapped it around the weasel's belly. He squeezed and smiled. The weasel struggled. Its black eyes bulged. It was caught in a viselike tongue-grip! Click, Chirp, and Crunch lifted their feet up high in the air, and promptly carried the weasel to the edge of the cliff. They blinked their warm, brown eyes at one another, swung the weasel out, and released it! The Twigs heard it spitting and snarling all the way to the jagged rocks below.

Leaf watched the evil creature fall, bounce off the boulders, and then slink away, wounded and defeated.

The stickytoes swaggered around the ledge and grinned hugely, with flat smiles from one ear to the other. Star rushed out and hugged each one, kissing each one between their eyes again and again. The babes tumbled from the shelter, giggling with excitement. Even Veil squeezed his way outside and slowly waved his hand. Joyfully, Veil's broad stripes turned various hues which reflected the morning sunrise.

Nervous about the noisy celebration, Leaf urged the babes to be quiet. Immediately, they grew solemn. Quickly, Star and Leaf moistened the stickytoes then packed the moss bags. Star strapped on the water-filled shells then tucked the babes into their cradles. Veil stepped onto his stick-sled and clung tightly. He was still glowing with the shades of the rose and orange sunrise. They started off at once.

Once again, Star trailed the procession. She continually searched for danger, especially for barkbiters. Leaf pulled Veil more easily as they traversed the ridge along its jagged crest. They no longer struggled uphill. The procession marched all morning and never rested. Soon the trail began to slope gently downward back toward the dying forest.

Much later in the day, Leaf stood on a large boulder and gazed south. Far away, over the tops of the brown, dying trees, Leaf spied the tips of the sugar pine trees. Before them, the ridgeline sank into the dying forest like the spine of a great beast. The log bridge was not far.

Leaf felt relieved that they were all still safe. *We'll be there by evening,* he thought. Hopefully Moon had reached Pappo in time. Leaf looked back at Star, waved to her, and smiled confidently.

Star sensed his optimistic mood, waved, and grinned back. Still uneasy however, she glanced over her shoulder.

Neither noticed the enormous beast trailing behind them, hidden in the shadow of the cliff.

CHAPTER EIGHTEEN

MOON

Moon was impatient, tired, and hungry. He was also irritated with the older Twigs who sat staring at him, their eggshell cups frozen midway to their lips. A slender, motherly Twig leaned against the wall, her mouth open and her eyes wide. She clutched her colorful leaf dress anxiously.

Moon spoke in a rush. "I've come to find Leaf's Pappo. Pesky brought me here to this old tree. Am I in the right knothole? Is PapaMook here?"

Mumma crossed the haven floor in one leap. She threw open her long, willowy arms and embraced the surprised Moon. "Yes, yes!" she cried. "You've come from the North Forest! You've seen Leaf! Is he all right?" Not waiting for an answer, she hugged him tight. She ignored Moon's wriggles as he squirmed to break free. "Mook is fine, dear little Twig," Mumma continued and patted Moon's head fondly. Finally, she released him. "He is sleeping now. Come. You must be hungry. Please sit here and eat." Mumma motioned to a space in the middle of the older Twigs.

Moon looked irritated at being called a little Twig, but hunger took over, and he allowed himself to be pushed gently to the floor. Mumma shoved a warm egg shell full of tea into his hands.

Sapper finally came to his senses. With one hand, he lifted a plate of berry mashcakes near Moon's head, and with the other hand, he offered him nutty pie. Moon drank his tea, dropped the shell on the floor, and stuffed his mouth full with no hesitation, or manners.

Pappo stepped quickly over to the knothole and peered out to check on Pesky. The tooler was there, happily yanking bugs from the bark, and gulping down worms. He was too busy poking his long, sharp beak into the deep furrows to notice Pappo.

Pappo looked back inside. He crossed his arms over his chest, stiffly planted his legs apart, and gazed with cool eyes at Moon, who continued to stuff cakes and pie in his already full mouth.

At last, Moon remembered to mumble, "Thank you, thank you."

The Cappynut Twigs murmured warm welcomes and encouraged him to eat and drink more. Mumma clasped and unclasped her hands. She stepped in between the Twigs and offered fluffy moss pillows for Moon to lean against.

It was then Pappo spoke in a deep, stern voice. "Moon, is it?"

All of the Twigs' mutters fell silent. They gazed at Pappo apprehensively.

With a frown, Pappo asked, "Where's Leaf?"

Moon swallowed, took another sip of tea, and said, "He's with Star and the babes. He's gonna guide them to the log that crosses the gorge. We have to go to the log bridge and help them across. Pesky knows the way."

The Twigs silently stared at Moon in disbelief.

Mumma sucked in her breath, and with a trembling voice, said, "A gorge? Cross a log over a gorge?" She stared at Pappo.

Pappo looked out of the knothole as if he could see the log from the Old Seeder. He only caught sight of Pesky pulling up a worm. Pappo turned back and blinked a few times at Moon. His mouth tightened. "Pesky? You say Pesky knows where this log is? And you say Leaf is guiding Twigs there?" Then Pappo slowly accented every word. "You say they are on their way there now?"

Moon looked very worried at Pappo's serious, angry questions. "We must meet them . . ." His voice trailed away at Pappo's glance. He stared down as if he had done something wrong.

Abruptly Sapper stood up and placed his hand on Pappo's shoulder. "No matter, no matter, old friend," he said. "I know where the gorge is. I'll lead us there and the tooler will find the log just as Moon said." Moon looked up hopefully.

Mumma and Pappo exchanged glances.

"Yes, yes!" piped up Ruffle and Tuffle. "We'll go to the gorge! We'll find the gorge! When do we go? When do we go?"

"All right, then. Fine. We'll go at dawn," Pappo said. He relaxed. The decision was made. He lifted Moon to his feet and placed both hands on his skinny shoulders.

In a kind voice, he said softly, "I'm sorry, Moon. I'm only angry with Leaf for flying off by himself. I should have thanked you first for coming to get us. You were right to come. We are in your debt."

Moon smiled broadly. "Don't worry. We'll find them." He nodded reassuringly.

"Now," Pappo slapped his hands together, "you must all get some sleep. We have soft moss beds here for Sapper and the twins. Moon, you can share Mook's bed in Leaf's hollow."

"Now, now, Needles. No fuss, no fuss," Sapper said firmly. "We'll all sleep on the branch outside. No problem. No problem. Come, Tuffle. Come now, Ruffle. Thank you, Ivy, for all the treats. We'll see you in the morning." They stepped through the knothole, and greeted Pesky with friendly interest.

Pesky froze, startled by the fluffy, multi-colored feathers of the Cappynut Twigs. He eyed them suspiciously, hopped backwards, and glared as if to warn them not to steal his worms.

Ruffle turned and waved good-naturedly to Moon as he left. "Rest well!" he said as they all disappeared into the leafy branches above.

"Moon," Mumma spoke gently, "come with me to Leaf's hollow. You can sleep on our fern blankets on the floor. Mook is still very weak. Mook will stay here with me, right, Pappo?" She looked sharply at Pappo for agreement. Pappo nodded.

"Moon?" a trembling voice spoke from the shadow just inside Leaf's hollow.

"Moon!" Mook cried out excitedly and staggered to him, arms wide. Moon jumped to Mook's embrace and they held each other tight for a long moment. Then Mook pushed him back and held his shoulders with his hands. "Star and the babes?" he said in an agonized voice.

Moon answered quickly. "They're fine, PapaMook. Leaf is bringing them here."

Mook turned at once to Pappo. "We must hurry to meet them! They'll need our help! They can't do it alone! We must hurry. . . . " Mook's voice faded as he sank to his knees, weak and faint.

Pappo and Mumma rushed to lift him back to Leaf's moss bed. "You must rest now, old Twig," Pappo said firmly. "We need to travel as fast as possible, and Whisper must carry food and water for us all. She cannot carry you. You must stay here and let Mumma make you well!" Pappo's voice had a no-nonsense tone.

Moon was very worried. He patted PapaMook's arm and soothed him. "Don't worry, PapaMook. We'll bring them back safe." He paused, then added, "Do they know about . . .?"

Mook answered Moon weakly. "They know everything." He turned his head away and sank into a deep, troubled sleep.

"What? What do we know?" Mumma asked, distressed.

"I'll tell you everything as we pack, Ivy," Pappo said quickly. "Now, Moon, you must rest too. Lie down here." At once Moon was put to bed on a pad of thick ferns.

Leaving the two to sleep, Mumma and Pappo sipped warm tea and sat close together on the floor. Pappo told her everything he knew about the dying forest and the Land of Dancing Sky Lights. Mumma cried with fear for Leaf.

At dawn, Mumma, Fern, Buddy, and Burba anxiously watched the forest floor from their high knothole halfway up the massive Old Seeder. Below, Pappo, Moon, Sapper, Ruffle, Tuffle, and Whisper faded into the sunlit flickers of the ancient trees. The group trotted north. Mumma felt a brush of wings as Pesky leapt from the nearby branch. The tooler spiraled into the pink morning sky and flew in lazy circles. He kept an eye on the Twigs' rustling shadows as they moved swiftly along a fox trail toward the Sharp Peaks. Pesky's wings glowed like fire in the sunrise as he patiently floated aloft.

Far away in the distance, across the great chasm, a thin wisp of smoke rose from a dying tree, curled into delicate strands, and faded into mist.

CHAPTER NINETEEN

COUGAR KITS PLAY

The sun burned hot on the ridge. The trail zigzagged between broken granite boulders which had fallen from the cliff and now lay cracked and scattered into pieces. Moss, Pool, Sand, Breeze, Cone, and Mist swayed in the cradles on Click, Chirp, and Crunch.

Leaf's shoulders ached. He shifted the rope loops trying to find some way to make them hurt less. He glanced back at Veil. The looksalot rolled his eyes and gripped the stick tightly.

Star trailed behind keeping a nervous watch. She grew more uneasy with each noise—a pebble rattling from the cliff or a hawk's scream. Star had felt disturbed all day. She sensed that some unseen danger lurked behind. Once, she thought she saw a huge shadow following behind them on the narrow trail. It was only a flickering shape in the corner of her eye but when she looked closely, it was not there. She checked on the babes, and felt reassured watching them play. They held out their tiny stick fingers and made shadow figures on the ground as they rode along. They giggled quietly at their hand-shadow creatures. Wavy hand- rabbits, chipmunks, and even an eagle floated on the trail beside the stickytoes. Pool still managed to cause trouble. He flew his hand-shadow into Sand's. He pretended it was a falcon hunting prey. Finally Pool actually attacked Sand's fingers, and she cried.

Star stepped up to their cradle and roughly tucked Pool's fingers into his lap. She frowned at him. "Pool, you must not hurt others. Please play a nice game!" she whispered sternly. He ignored her. Star patted Sand's hand and wiped away her tears. She caught Leaf's eye as he glanced back and waved to let him know all was well. Suddenly she felt as if someone—or something— watched her. Star checked over her shoulder again. She peered intently into the cracks in the granite cliff. She wished she felt all *was* well.

In a dry, sandy cave higher up the cliff, three cougar kits played with their shadows, too. They leapt from narrow ledges along the cave wall and tried to catch their twitching tail shadows on the soft, sandy floor. The fluffy kits tumbled, rolled, and pounced on each other. They had already filled their bellies with sweet milk and now they stalked their shadows as they practiced their hunting skills.

A tiny shadow leapt from a rock into the cave. An unsuspecting, long-legged cricket hopped in a jerky zigzag between the delighted kits. At once, all three kits leapt on it, smothering it with their downy fur. The cricket popped up between their pudgy bodies, and landed on a pink nose. The startled kit crossed her eyes at the cricket which promptly made a magnificent high leap straight out of the cave.

Nearby, their mum stretched out on her side in the sun. She yawned and closed her copper-colored eyes. It was time to nap. The kits' blue eyes blinked at one another. What mischief might they discover while their mum slept? They crept across the sand as if they stalked an injured, flapping bird, but soon they tired of that game.

What was beyond their world? The kits peeked over the edge of their high cave. Their fluffy rust-speckled coats blended in with the sunbeams that skittered across the granite walls. Only their bright blue eyes gave them away.

The tiny cougar kits stared curiously at the rocky trail below. A strange procession traversed the ridge. A weird stick creature pulled a large, grayish colored thing with rolling eyes on a long stick. Behind them were three wet-looking, orange-spotted stickytoes carrying many tiny stick creatures on their backs. Last, a skinny stick creature with silvery, leafy hair followed them all.

The three kits' watched intently. Their stiff, fuzzy tails switched in the sand behind them in unison—back and forth, back and forth. Their blue eyes widened. Their ears laid back. Their bodies trembled with excitement. At once, the kits crept over the edge of the cave and slid down to get a better look. Their tiny claws scraped the loose rocks, and pebbles fell to the trail below. Their mum slept peacefully . . . unaware.

Suddenly, the kits tumbled over one another down the cliff face until they landed clumsily in a confused heap right in front of a very surprised Leaf. He held up his hand at once. The march abruptly stopped. The sticky-toes bumped into one another and trampled on each others' tails. Star scrambled quickly up the trail around the stickytoes to see what was wrong. She saw the clump of fuzzy, blue-eyed balls of furry kits, and grinned.

The cougar kits untangled their little bodies, rolled around on the trail, and bumped into one another. Leaf and Star burst out laughing. Restrained in the carry-cradles, the babes stretched against their belts to get a better view.

The kits growled—it was more like mewing—and scratched the dirt with teeny claws. They were already taller than Star but now they puffed up to twice their size, hissed fiercely at the Twigs, and bared their tiny, bright teeth. Clumsily, they attempted a sideways rush at Leaf.

Fearlessly, Star held up her hand. The kits skidded to a stop in surprise. She touched their pink noses. "Here now, little ones. We won't hurt you," she said soothingly. "Have you lost your mum?"

At that very moment, a deafening, furious howl echoed down the cliff. Terrified, the Twigs looked up and saw an enormous, bristling silhouette of a cougar atop a large boulder. They were horrified. It was the kits' mum, and she was very angry.

She stood rigid. Her powerful shoulders rippled. Her claws clicked and scratched the granite. Her eyes glared suspiciously as she examined the scene below. Snarling and spitting, she narrowed her eyes, preparing to attack. The cougar mum's shadow fell over the trembling Twigs, stickytoes, and looksalot.

The Twig babes screamed and hid in their cradles. Veil instinctively turned the color of dirt. Click, Chirp, and Crunch froze, each with one foot dangling midair. Star cringed. Leaf, stumbled back, shrank against Veil, and hoped he was invisible.

With their mum's arrival, the kits' courage returned. Once again, they bounced sideways at Leaf. They reached out with their tiny claws and slapped at Star's silver, leafy hair.

Star hopped backward and screamed, "Stop it!" Then she quickly looked up at the terrifying mum. Desperately, she yelled, "We won't hurt them! They're attacking us!"

"Hush," said Leaf, throwing his arm in front of her protectively. "Don't you see she doesn't care if we're not hurting her kits? Be quiet and stop moving!"

"How can I not move?" Star cried as she dodged the claws and covered her head with her hands. "The kits are trying to yank my hair out!"

In a flash of bristling fur, the kits' mum landed on the trail directly before Leaf. Her growl was like deep, rumbling thunder. Her fangs sparkled and her eyes were flames.

Star and Leaf cowered in her hot breath. They closed their eyes and sank on the trail, too weak with fear to stand.

The cougar mum roared! The ghastly sound split the air. She raised her deadly claws, curled and ready to strike.

Just then, a deafening rumble echoed off the granite cliff. It was shattering! Even more horrified, Star and Leaf opened their eyes in spite of their fear. A great, white spirit bear angrily rushed up the steep trail behind them. Her golden-tipped fur spiked stiff on her shoulders. When she reached the stickytoes, she rose up on her powerful back legs, flung spit from her teeth, ripped the air over the Twig babes with huge, black claws, and roared as if an avalanche were crashing down from the rocky crest upon them all.

Terrified, the cougar mum cowered on the trail, and pushed the kits behind her with one swipe of her huge paw. The Twigs crouched between the cougar mum and the furious spirit bear. Deafening roars and spitting snarls shook the ground.

Star and Leaf held their hands over their ears. The babes screamed. The stickytoes and looksalot froze in fear.

The two mighty beasts raged at one another!

Star and Leaf held onto each other, helpless, weak and trembling, their eyes squeezed shut so tight, they hurt.

Unexpectedly the cougar mum spun swiftly around and shoved her kits up the cliff. She glanced over her shoulder and spit a fierce, warning threat at the spirit bear not to follow. Snarling, she thrust the clumsy kits up through the loose rocks until at last, they all disappeared over the ledge into their shadowy cave. Her angry growls continued, but now she was chastising her kits for their wicked escapade.

The spirit bear dropped onto her enormous paws and stared intently at the Twigs. With an odd expression, Star stood up and stared just as intently at the bear. Her eyes cleared of terror and, to Leaf's amazement, she lifted her hand and waved. Then she laughed and waved both arms above her head as if exchanging an excited, happy greeting with the gigantic beast.

Leaf was stunned. "What are you doing?" he cried out, terribly alarmed. "It's a bear!"

"No, Leaf, don't you see?" Star answered joyfully as she hopped up and down. "She saved us! It's one of PapaMook's spirit bear cubs that he rescued in the West Forest! She's all grown up! She remembers PapaMook!"

"Remembers . . . ?" Leaf's voice trailed off, confused. He backed away and hid behind Veil.

The looksalot watched Star curiously as she jumped up and down.

Leaf peeked over Veil's back. He had never heard of Twigs befriending bears before. And this was no ordinary bear. She was huge! And scary! Still, Leaf had to admit, she was magnificent, too. Gold dust sparkled on the tips of her white fur like a hazy, glowing sunset. Awestruck, Leaf stood up. His fear disappeared. *A spirit bear had saved them! And incredibly, PapaMook is her friend!*

The gigantic beast rose up again, and waved her black paws around in the air as if returning Star's greeting. She shook her massive head up and down then fell heavily onto her front paws. She turned awkwardly on the narrow trail and lumbered away. As she tramped along, her shaggy, golden-tipped shoulders rippled as if she were pleased with Star's gratitude and the memory of an old friend. She disappeared around a granite slab. Her contented grunts faded away.

Star turned to Leaf and grinned. "She's one of PapaMook's bear cubs from the West Forest!"

"Yes," answered Leaf. "You said that." Still, a little skeptical, however, he glanced sideways at Star. He lifted the loops of the stick-sled over his shoulders. Leaf rolled his eyes at Veil.

Veil rolled his eyes at Leaf.

Star kissed each babe and stickytoes sweetly then happily took up her position at the rear of the procession. She smiled to herself each time she looked back to where the spirit bear had stood. Her face glowed and her eyes twinkled. "It wasn't just a story," she whispered cheerfully to the back of the Twig babes' heads. They twisted in their seats to catch her words. "PapaMook really did save the spirit bear cubs in the cedar den just like he said!" Star smiled at them lovingly. "Wait until we tell PapaMook one of his spirit bear cubs saved our lives! Wait until we tell Moon!" Then her smile faded as worry replaced her joy.

Star looked ahead at the downward sloping trail. She hoped PapaMook and Moon were safe. She hoped she would see their dear, silly Pesky soon. Most of all, she hoped they would cross safely over the log bridge to the South Forest.

Star glanced over her shoulder and unexpectedly shivered. Once more she felt something was very, very wrong—that something horrible chased them.

CHAPTER TWENTY

PESKY'S PLAN

Pappo, Moon, and the Cappynut Twigs trotted with Whisper along the wide forest paths.

Moon glimpsed curiously at Ruffle and Tuffle's long feathers fanned out behind them and stuck into their belts. One of Tuffle's feathers hung so long, it brushed the ground behind him as he ran. Finally, Moon pointed to one of Tuffle's feathers. "What's that for?" he asked.

Tuffle grinned, but it was Ruffle who answered. "Listen," he said and quickly whipped out his own long feather from its back loop. Ruffle held the feather to his lips and blew through a hole punched in the thin, hollow bone. A beautiful melody echoed all around them.

Moon's eyes lit up. "Excellent!" he cried out. "Could you teach me to do that?"

"Sure!" Ruffle and Tuffle answered together.

Tuffle added, "We'll find you a feather right away. You'll need more than one to disguise yourself, you know!"

"Blue jay feathers are best!" declared Ruffle.

"No, no, Moon. You must use thrush feathers," corrected Tuffle.

"No. A blue jay's," repeated Ruffle.

"A thrush is better!" argued Tuffle.

They paused for a moment to glare at one another then shrugged and sprinted after the others.

Moon wondered how blue or yellow feathers could help a Twig hide in the green moss or a tree. He eyed the twins' feathers doubtfully. They looked like a couple of crazy birds hopping down the forest trail. Moon thought wryly that the only way they'd blend in is if they sat in a bird nest.

Tuffle pulled one of his yellow feathers out of his belt and pushed it through Moon's strap. "Don't you just feel like a bird now?" he asked.

"Uh, sure," Moon answered. He tugged the feather sideways, so he wouldn't trip.

Pappo held Whisper's rope, and briskly led the small group. They had traveled all morning and now the shadows stretched toward midday.

Pappo halted the march, held his hand over his eyes, and squinted at the sky. Abruptly he said, "Let's rest."

The Twigs plopped onto the moss at once.

Pappo gazed at Pesky, circling above. "How are we supposed to know if Pesky is leading us anywhere?" he asked Sapper. "It looks like he's just following us. He's not leading us to the log at all."

Sapper looked up and watched the tooler circle around for a moment then shrugged. "I don't know what he's doing. He's your friend's tooler. Didn't he tell you how to read tooler signs?"

"Well, you're the bird expert," Pappo retorted, exasperated with Sapper's unhelpful response.

Sapper studied Pesky's slow spirals again, and frowned. "Well, I guess we're headed toward the log bridge alright, or he'd screech at us or something."

Pappo stared skeptically at Sapper then shook his head. "At least you can get us to the gorge." He glanced up at Pesky. "Then we'll see if that nutty tooler knows which direction to go from there." Irritated, he yanked some seeds out of Whisper's backpack, and tossed a few in his mouth. He unhooked a cappynut, hastily gulped some water, and shoved a capful under Whisper's nose.

Suddenly, Pesky dove at his head. His wings nearly knocked Pappo over. Obviously, the tooler wanted his share of the treats, too. He spun back around, skipped across the moss, tripped over a root, and accidentally whacked Whisper's tail with his wing as he slid by. The usually sweet chipmunk glared a warning at the clumsy tooler.

"Well, he doesn't have any problem telling us he wants something to eat," Pappo muttered under his breath. He tossed a berry to Pesky who gulped it down before it touched the ground. Pappo patted Whisper's head soothingly. She glowered at Pesky. Pappo sipped more water, ate a few more seeds then hastily packed the food back in Whisper's pack. "We must hurry on," he announced.

The others looked surprised. "We've hardly rested at all!" Ruffle exclaimed. Then he saw the worried expression on Pappo's face. Ruffle nodded to the others. Silently, the Cappynut Twigs readied themselves for another brisk jog through the forest.

Pesky hopped down the mossy path, launched an awkward, lopsided leap, and flew directly into a

low-hanging branch. The Twigs watched in astonishment as Pesky's black wings beat against the pinecones
and needles furiously as if he were trying to beat the tree
to death. Suddenly, Pesky dropped on the tree roots. A
fat, purplish caterpillar hung from his long beak. The
frantic bug wriggled desperately, its many teeny legs
raced away in the air, but Pesky whacked it on a stone
to stun it, and quickly gulped it down with a satisfied
smirk. After that, he glared at the Twigs, hopped away
from the roots, and then swiftly flew up above the treetops. With outstretched wings he circled high above the
Twigs once again.

The Twigs rolled their eyes at one another. *Toolers!*

Swiftly, they raced off, following the well-trodden
path once more. As they ran, the sun climbed higher,
and their shadows grew shorter before them.

After a while, Sapper called out to Pappo, "Don't
worry, Needles. At this pace, we'll be to the chasm
before a bird can build a nest!"

Just at that moment, a fat pine tree cone fell on the
path near Pappo's feet. It bounced on the trail and
smacked into a puffy mushroom. Pappo automatically
looked up. It was early in the season for cones to be
dropping. *Where did it fall from?* Strangely, a pebble

suddenly whizzed past his nose, struck a stone near Sapper, and barely missed Ruffle's head as it bounced past the young Twig.

Pappo hastily held up his arms to signal a stop. "Watch out!" he yelled as a clump of moss plummeted toward Whisper. He ducked into the tangled roots of a massive cedar tree. The others rushed in, crowding the small space.

Unexpectedly, Moon laughed, pointed up at the sky, and said, "Look! It's just Pesky!"

Pesky's shadow flowed over the path toward the Twigs and Whisper. He carried a huge, white, mushroom in his mouth. He flung it from his beak directly at the roots where the Twigs crouched. The mushroom burst into tiny, bright pieces as it struck the tree trunk just above their heads.

"He's trying to tell us something!" Moon shouted excitedly. "Look!"

Pesky spiraled very high. His wings spread out stiff and straight. Then he tilted his entire body to the right, leveled out, then tilted right again. He whistled shrilly to the Twigs below.

"We must go right!" Moon shouted, "Right!" He was thrilled Pesky had not failed them. "Right! We need to go right!"

"Right is right!" yelled Ruffle.

Tuffle looked surprised at his brother's shout, but only for a moment. The twins grinned at one and at once took up the cheery cry.

"Right is right! We must go right!" Ruffle and Tuffle chanted in unison. "Right is right! We must go right!" The twins marched around a mossy stone, their steps high and exaggerated, their knobby knees nearly thumping their skinny chests. "Right is right! We must go right!" Their noses looked like sharp bird beaks stabbing the air.

"Alright, alright, already!" Pappo yelled above the frightful clamor. "We'll go right!" He hoped his words would stop Ruffle and Tuffle's annoying march. He crawled from the roots at once, stood with his hands on his hips, and scanned the nearby blackberry thickets for a clear path to follow.

"Thanks, Pesky," Moon called out. He waved to the tooler gratefully as Pesky returned to circling slowly above the tree tops, reassured the Twigs understood his demands to go right.

Soon Pappo spotted a partially hidden deer trail which pushed through the thick, thorny brambles. "We'll follow this trail," Pappo stated flatly.

Sapper, Ruffle, and Tuffle exchanged glances. Blackberry brambles often hid many creatures—many of which were unfriendly to Twigs, such as snakes and skunks. Worst of all, sweet blackberries attract bears. Most Twigs avoid these thickets.

But Pappo walked directly into the bushes without a backward glance. Whisper hesitated for only a moment, but with a gentle tug at her rope, Pappo led her confidently behind him. At once, Moon followed.

The others followed Pappo more slowly. They peered cautiously into the tangle of twisted stems, wary and alert for any movement.

Pesky whistled sharply from the sky as if to say, *That's right! To the right!*

"Do you think he sees the log already?" Moon whispered to the Cappynut Twigs.

"Well, he sees something for sure," Sapper answered quietly. "Hey, Needles," he called out in a low voice to Pappo. "Don't you think birds are the smartest creatures in the forest now?"

"Sure," Pappo grumbled, "just as long as he doesn't whack us with a rock to get our attention!" He glanced up suspiciously in case Pesky *was* aiming a rock at his head.

The Twigs cautiously made their way through the blackberry thicket. Soon they burst into a sunny, grassy meadow. Pappo's pace quickened as he continued to follow the deer trail.

"So where are we going now?" asked Ruffle and Tuffle as they hurried to match Pappo's pace.

"To the log, my fine, young Twigs," answered Sapper cheerfully. "We're off to the log!"

CHAPTER TWENTY-ONE

GLOW ON THE RIDGE

"We'll be there soon!" Sapper yelled to Ruffle and Tuffle as he encouraged them to keep pace with Pappo's long stride.

Moon ran beside Pappo who was intent only on the path before them. The younger Twig glanced around, eager to spot the gorge. Suddenly, Moon stopped in the middle of the trail which brought a halt to the whole procession. Sapper, Ruffle, and Tuffle slammed into him and knocked Moon into the grass.

Irritated with the twins, Moon stood up and briskly brushed himself off.

"Why'cha stop?" asked Ruffle curiously.

"Look!" Moon pointed up at a towering sugar pine tree beside the trail. It was so tall it appeared to be falling on top of them. The sun burned through its thin needles. The Twigs blinked rapidly in the sunlight as they all looked up.

Moon frowned at them. "Look!" he said again and pointed at the tree's tip. "Up there! It's Pesky! He's just sitting up there!"

Sapper and Pappo shielded their eyes from the sun and stared up at the top of the tree. Pesky was difficult to spot but after the Twigs tilted their heads back and forth a few times the tooler's silhouette appeared. He perched as if frozen, rigidly clutching a high branch. He seemed to be staring in the direction of the North Forest.

"What is it?" asked Moon. "Why isn't he flying?"

Pappo and Moon looked questioningly at Sapper, the self-proclaimed bird expert. He only shrugged. "I don't know," he said sheepishly.

"Oh, just great!" exclaimed Pappo. "Now I'll have to climb up there and find out what's the matter with Pesky!"

"I'm coming too!" said Moon.

"Just stay here with the others," said Pappo in a gruff, irritated voice.

Moon stepped boldly in front of Pappo. He put his hands on his hips, scowled, and with a determined voice, said, "I'm coming too."

Surprised, Pappo frowned at the young Twig but then his face softened. "Of course, Moon. You should come, too. I'm sorry. Climb up with me. I'm sure your sharp eyes will be of great help." Pappo motioned for Moon to start up the tree first.

The others made themselves comfortable in the deep moss of the sugar pine tree's roots. Whisper shrugged off the pack from her back and curled up in a tight, fuzzy ball to take a nap. The Cappynut Twigs leaned back against their soft feathers, and at once were fast asleep.

Pappo grinned at Moon, "Looks like we won't be missed much."

Moon grinned back. He was relieved Pappo seemed friendly again.

They quickly ascended the towering tree. "Have you climbed this high before?" Pappo asked Moon kindly. They moved swiftly from branch to branch as they talked.

"No," admitted Moon. "I'm a good climber though!"

"Well, as long as you keep a tight grip, you've nothing to worry about!" Pappo said encouragingly. "Tall trees are like any other tree. You just climb farther up."

Moon smiled at him. He had missed his own papps enormously but had kept those feelings deeply buried. The noonday sun streamed through the fragrant pine needles. Moon felt warm and comforted by Pappo's interest in him. He began to say something to Pappo, then unexpectedly choked up, sat down, and began to cry.

Pappo understood at once. He sat beside Moon, encircled the young Twig's shaking shoulders with his long, skinny arm, and patted Moon's white, leafy head. After a long while, the young Twig's ragged weeping turned to sniffles.

Pappo said gently, "You will always have a haven with us, Moon. You and Star and PapaMook and the Twig babes can live here in this beautiful South Forest. Your home is with us now."

Moon nodded gratefully and smiled weakly.

"Now," Pappo slapped his knee. "The day isn't flowing any slower! Let's finish this climb and find out what's bothering your silly old tooler!"

"Let's go, then!" Moon laughed.

As they reached the highest tip where Pesky perched, Pappo realized something was very wrong. Pesky clutched the thin limb as if frozen. He shivered fearfully as if absolutely terrified.

The Twigs looked where Pesky stared. At first Pappo and Moon's astonished gaze was fixed only on the great chasm below which brutally cut the forest in two. But then, horrified, they saw it!

A firestorm stalked the North Forest!

Far away, flames snaked through the tree branches and burst from their tips. Forest creatures fled before the smoke which rolled toward the gorge. Deer ran panic-stricken up to the edge of a terrifying chasm, then turned and raced perilously along its edge.

Where were they going? Pappo stretched in the tree top to see better but couldn't. Trees even taller than the sugar pine blocked his view. Moon clasped hold of his leg, frightened that Pappo would fall. Pappo couldn't see it, but he somehow knew the creatures were racing to the log bridge.

"Pesky." Pappo tried to soothe the frightened tooler. "You don't need to come any farther. It's all right. I know where the log is now. I can take us there. You've been a great help to us. You must fly away and stay safe. Thank you, Pesky. You're a wonderful tooler!"

Pesky blinked and peered intently into Pappo's eyes. Grateful the old Twig had released him from his vital mission, the tooler dove from the tree's tip and soared swiftly away—far away from the fire.

"You can't blame him for flying away," Moon explained to Pappo sadly. "Birds are terribly afraid of fire. Look over there." Moon pointed to the sky above the stabbing, golden flames.

Birds of all shapes and sizes flew from the choking smoke. It didn't matter what they were—hawks, ravens, swallows, or swifts—they all flocked together like a dark, rolling wave to escape the flames.

Moon tried to defend his friend. "Pesky got us to the log bridge, though. He helped us this far."

"Yes," Pappo reassured Moon. "We couldn't have found the log without him." Pappo couldn't help but ask Moon, "Do you see Leaf or Star or the babes anywhere?"

Moon clung to a thin branch and stretched as tall as he dared. Pappo held his skinny legs to keep him steady. "No, I can't see them." Moon replied. "But they'll be moving in the same direction as all the other creatures, I'm sure. Wait! Look!"

"What do you see?" Pappo grabbed Moon's shoulder strap, worried the young Twig would fall.

Moon shouted, "There's the stickytoes!"

"What? Stickytoes?" Pappo squinted to see. "Those barkhuggers? You call them stickytoes?"

Moon was very excited now. "It's Star's stickytoes. And look! They're carrying the babes on their backs!"

Moon and Pappo studied the tiny figures across the enormous chasm. Three stickytoes squatted beside two Twigs. A swaying looksalot clung to a forked stick nearby. They all huddled together on a giant slab which hung out over the gorge. Oddly, they looked as if they were having a picnic!

"It's Leaf!" cried out Pappo.

"It's Star!" shouted Moon. "There they are!" Moon screamed Star's name and waved his arms so violently, Pappo was afraid he'd fling himself from the branches of the towering tree.

"Stop, Moon! Stop!" urged Pappo. "They can't hear us from here." Pappo suddenly looked very worried. "We must get to the log, Moon! I don't think they see the fire! They don't seem to know that they're in danger! Moon, we must warn them!"

Pappo tugged his whistletube from its loop and blasted a piercing, shrill note.

Far across the gorge, Leaf paused from munching on seeds and turned at the sound. He stood and stared at the tree across the chasm where Moon and Pappo clung to the high limbs. Immediately he drew his whistletube from its loop and blew a lovely answering melody back. Leaf caught sight of Moon waving his arms at the top of the giant sugar pine. He and Star began jumping and shouting excitedly. They waved back.

Moon screamed and pointed behind them at the approaching fire. His voice was lost over the gorge.

Leaf, Star, and the babes simply waved happily.

"They don't understand," cried Moon in despair. "How can we tell them to run? How can we make them see the fire?"

"Climb down! We must go to the log!" cried Pappo. "Leaf will realize there's a fire soon enough when he smells the smoke and sees the creatures running before it!"

Swiftly, they dropped from branch to branch. Halfway down the giant tree, Moon and Pappo started shouting at the Cappynut Twigs and Whisper to wake up and prepare to leave. They dropped through the tree limbs and yelled about the fire, the need for speed, and that they must meet Leaf at the log. Moon and Pappo fell with a clumsy, heavy thud onto the soft moss in the roots of the tree. The Cappynut Twigs and Whisper stood ready to leave.

Without another word the Twigs raced off. Anxiously, Pappo and Moon led the way to the log bridge. As they raced to the gorge, they hurtled roots, splashed through shallow creeks, tripped over ivy vines, and burst through blackberry thickets without slowing their pace. Whisper hopped behind, carrying her own braided rope in her mouth.

Pappo's eyes stared beyond the brambles. He didn't care whether the Cappynut Twigs and Whisper kept pace now or not.

Moon ran beside him, silent and swift.

Both envisioned the gold flames leaping into the blue sky behind Leaf and Star. Both imagined the churning gray smoke and the suffocating cloud spreading toward the chasm. They thought of the terrified creatures, panicked and stumbling toward the log bridge, their only path to safety.

The dry needles, brittle cones, withered limbs, and rotten wood of the infested North Forest had unleashed a scorching, deadly sky of fire.

SKY OF FIRE

 ϵ arlier that afternoon, Leaf and Star slid down a steep hillside through loose gravel. They had left the scraggly, twisted bristle cone pine trees of the barren rocks behind them. They followed the spine of the ridge as it sank into the flat forest floor. The trees grew tall around them once again. The monolithic fir trees cut the sky like spears as the Twigs entered the brown paths of the dying forest.

Star and Leaf glanced at each other, worried. They crept as silent as flittering butterflies among the trees, but the danger of a barkbiter attack was more likely with each step.

Working as one, Leaf and Star now pulled Veil together. Chirp, Click, and Crunch swayed ahead of them and lightly bounced the Twig babes as they jogged along, to the delight of the tiny babes.

With many whispers Star urged the stickytoes to slow down, but instead, excited by the stifled giggles of the babes, the stickytoes ran faster and soon outpaced her. Leaf and Star lost sight of them as they dashed down a path into a patch of twisting, dry thickets.

Star anxiously shouted after them. "Wait for us!"

Hastily, Leaf grabbed her arm to still her cry as the stickytoes disappeared into the bushes. The giggles of the babes faded away.

Leaf and Star tried to pull Veil's sled faster, but the sticks sank into the dead needles and bunched up around Veil's spiral tail. The looksalot rolled his eyes in alarm and turned a dusty shade of brown similar to the brittle pine needles. The dagger-like needles could easily pierce his scales, so Leaf and Star were forced to slow their pace. They followed the trail which led into the thickets.

After a breathless sprint, Leaf and Star burst through the prickly bushes where the stickytoes had vanished, and found themselves on a flat granite slab. It stuck out right over the terrifyingly deep chasm, and hung there precariously. Only blue sky defined where the slab ended and the chasm began.

"Stop!" screamed Leaf. He fell back and dug his feet into the granite to stop the sled from sliding forward.

Star fell past him, twisted around, and frantically pushed Veil back with her feet to keep him from tumbling over the edge.

Leaf froze—suddenly overwhelmed by the dizzying sight—sheer multicolored granite walls rose up before a sickeningly unnatural empty space. He realized at once that the stickytoes would have sensed the open space and avoided this dangerous drop to nothing. He and Star needed to return to the thickets and find the path the stickytoes had taken. He yanked at the ropes to turn Veil's sled around.

Star sank trembling onto the slab, rocked back and forth with her arms around her knees, and sobbed, "Oh, no, we've lost them! They're gone! Oh, Leaf, they've fallen over the cliff!"

"Star," Leaf murmured softly and knelt beside her. He put his arm around her shoulders. "Star, they haven't fallen over the edge, if that's what you are thinking. The stickytoes are too smart for that!"

Star took her hands from her teary face and looked in disbelief at him. "But I saw them! They ran straight this way! I saw them!" she cried.

"No, no, Star," Leaf soothed her. "They would have sensed this drop-off. The babes could not have been better protected. They took another path back in the thickets someplace. Come, now, we must find them!" Leaf stood up, confident he was right. To encourage her, he stood with his hands on his hips, and peered into the tangled bushes right behind them.

Star looked hopeful. Then her face brightened. "Leaf," she called out with a surprisingly cheerful voice. "I know where they are! Wait a moment. Be still!" she commanded.

Startled, Leaf waited. Just in case there was danger, Veil turned gray.

Star stepped slowly up to the edge of the thickets. She turned in exaggerated circles with her arms outstretched, and spoke in a loud, merry, sing-song cadence. "Oh my! Where have the Twig babes gone? I don't see them anywhere. Where have they gone? I only see bushes and rocks and sticks here. Where have the babes gone?"

Leaf frowned. "What are you doing?"

Star grinned slyly at Leaf, winked, and continued to ask her sing-song questions to the air. "Oh, dear, where did the babes go? Where could they be?"

Suddenly, giggles erupted.

Quickly, Star stepped lightly over to a sweet-smelling huckleberry bush, peeked through its leaves, and laughed. "Leaf, look!"

Giggles burst from the bush. Little hands clapped with delight at being found. Tiny voices chirped, "We were trees! You couldn't find us! We were trees!"

The stickytoes stepped from the tangled bush with huge, wide grins on their faces.

"Star, you found us! We were hiding!" The tiny babes giggled even more.

Star chuckled and answered, "Yes, you were trees. Excellent trees! You sure had us fooled! Weren't they amazing trees, Leaf?"

Leaf grinned weakly and nodded.

"Come on now, you silly babes! It's time to have treats and rest awhile." She laughed, relieved the babes were safe. They crouched together on the slab, and munched on dried berries.

As they enjoyed their picnic at the edge of the chasm, a piercing whistle suddenly sliced the air around them.

Leaf recognized the urgent, familiar note at once. Pappo's whistletube! He stood and scanned the trees across the gorge.

"Star look! It's Moon and Pappo! There, in the top of that tall tree across the canyon!"

"Oh, look!" Star cried happily to the babes. "Look! It's Moon!" The babes giggled, cooed, and waved cheerfully to Moon. Star laughed. "Look at him wave! Moon is so excited to see us! Is Pesky there, too? I don't see him. I wonder where he is?"

Leaf looked carefully at the treetops surrounding Pappo and Moon, and he searched the sky above them. "Nope, I don't see Pesky either. Well, he'll show up, I'm sure. So, do you want to rest some more here or just go on to the log bridge?" Leaf asked, already knowing her answer.

"Oh, let's go on," Star nodded eagerly. "They're going to meet us there, I'm sure. What do you think, little babes? Should we go on to the bridge?" They all nodded vigorously.

Leaf looked back at the tree top and saw Pappo and Moon climbing down. "Looks like they are already on their way to the log," Leaf told Star.

Quickly, Star and Leaf lifted the babes into their stickytoes cradles. Star glanced at the sheer drop-off uneasily. She tied the babes' shoulder straps very tightly, made sure each babe was snugly seated, patted their heads, and kissed each cheek. Then she briefly pressed her cheek to each stickytoes.

Leaf watched her preparations patiently.

Star brushed her hands over Veil's scales to be sure he was ready to continue the trek. The pleased looksalot turned green and blue at her touch.

Finally, Star turned to Leaf and said, "We're all set, but this time, let's stick together!"

"I agree," said Leaf simply. "You walk up front this time. I'll pull Veil behind all of you. That way you can catch the stickytoes if they take off again!"

Star nodded. Cautiously, she led the stickytoes along the edge of the gorge on a treacherous, narrow trail. Soon they reached a point where they could see the incredible length of the chasm.

They paused to admire the fantastic view, cheerful that the end of their journey was so near. As they shared a cappynut shell of water and some seeds, Star stared in awe at the beautiful, dark green South Forest across the gorge.

"See, little ones," Star said sweetly to the Twig babes. She swept her arm toward the south rim. "There are all the green trees I told you about!"

For fun, Leaf threw a stone over the side of the cliff. Star counted slowly to ten before they saw it disappear into the white rapids of the turbulent river far below.

"That's a long way down," Leaf said a little nervously. "I sure hope that log is strong enough for us to get across safely." Leaf touched Star's elbow and pointed farther up the canyon.

There it was! Their crossing point—a massive cedar tree which had toppled from the South Forest to the North Forest, across the chasm, long ago. It gripped the south rim with its tangled, knotty roots and held fast to the north rim with gnarled, branches which clutched at boulders like gigantic fists.

Star stared in amazement at the enormous, dead tree bridging the deep cut in the earth. First, she felt sad for the mighty, ancient tree. Next, she felt afraid. *They would never make it across!*

Leaf climbed on top of a large boulder which partially blocked their trail. "I'll just check to see how much further it is," he told Star although he was really just excited to see if Pappo had already reached the log.

The boulder was the highest point on the narrow path to the sugar pine trees. A light breeze ruffled

Leaf's green, leafy hair. His eyes blinked in the bright, hot sun.

"Look at that," he said to Star, sounding a little bewildered. "Look at all the creatures racing across the log bridge. That's really weird."

"What did you say?" asked Star. She looked up and shielded the sun from her eyes with both of her slender, brown hands. She had just finished dripping water all over the stickytoes— from their noses to the ends of their tails. She sprinkled the babes too, just for fun.

A deer suddenly leapt past them, its eyes glazed.

At once, a horrible feeling swept over Leaf. Quickly, he looked behind him at the North Forest and sucked in his breath. Immediately, he reached to pull Star up beside him.

"What is it?" Star cried out, instantly alarmed. She grabbed Leaf's outstretched hand.

Speechless, Leaf lifted her onto the boulder then pointed to the high crest of the ridge where they had been earlier that day.

Billowing, gray ashes curled above it. Within the thick, swirling clouds, gold and orange flames danced madly, and whirled dry needles into a spinning whip until they sizzled into ash.

At that same moment, Star and Leaf smelled smoke and heard the fierce, sucking wind of the forest fire. Burning limbs crashed far away and echoed off the walls of the gorge.

A firestorm!

CHAPTER TWENTY-THREE

PANIC AT THE GORGE

Leaf slid down the boulder. He braced himself against it as he struggled to breathe. *Fire!*

Star stood trembling. "Oh no!" she gasped, horrified, and in the next instant, she cried out, "How far is the log?"

Leaf choked on his words. "We must run!"

Star swallowed hard. She turned and hurried to the stickytoes, pulled the babes' shoulder ropes even tighter, quickly kissed each one, and sternly ordered, "Hold on! We're going to run!"

The Twig babes sat wide-eyed. They sensed Star was serious. It was not a game.

Leaf watched as she whispered to Crunch, Chirp, and Click to move very fast but be careful of the cliff edge.

The stickytoes and Veil lifted their noses high. They now smelled the smoke, too, and understood Star's urgency. They knew a forest fire was moving quickly toward them.

Leaf noticed Veil was very pale so he patted his nose and whispered, "Just hang on, Veil."

Star stepped beside Leaf and said firmly, "I'll help pull Veil." She turned and kissed Veil on his scaly nose, then slipped one of the loops over her shoulder. Leaf slipped on the other loop and they took the lead.

At first they slipped on the loose rocks and had to brace themselves to keep from falling over the cliff. So they moved again more slowly, this time very careful of their footing. Finally the trail veered away from the chasm's edge, and Leaf and Star could sprint faster toward the log bridge. The stickytoes ran close behind.

Panicked forest creatures overtook them on the trail. Deer, squirrels, rabbits, raccoons, and even an evil weasel raced past them toward the log. Frantic and desperate, they fled before the crackling sparks and hot ash that were already showering the path.

"The fire is coming this way!" Star stuttered with fear. She glanced back and stumbled.

"Run faster!" commanded Leaf and strained against the sled's rope. The stickytoes suddenly shot past Leaf and rushed toward the bridge.

"Go to the log!" Star shouted at them. Then she caught her breath. The cougar mum and her kits streaked past, looking neither right nor left. A family of skunks quickly waddled by. None of the forest creatures even glanced at one another, only intent on leaping, hopping, padding and scrambling as fast as they could before the terror that was devouring the forest behind them.

Leaf heard a crash. He looked back and saw a blazing fir tree fall to the earth with a mighty roar. Burning scarlet spikes streaked up the trunks of trees nearby and set their dead branches aflame.

"Oh, Leaf!" Star strangled on the words. "Fire!" It was a Twig's worst fear.

Leaf took her elbow with one hand, grasped the rope's loop with the other, and urgently yanked her and Veil along at the same pace. At last Star, Leaf, and Veil staggered into twisted, thick creeper vines. They covered the boulders which anchored the mighty tree's topmost branches to the north rim. The knotty tangles formed a cool cave which led into the old tree's damp hollow trunk.

They had reached the log bridge!

Swiftly, Leaf tugged Veil into the embrace of the vines—deep in the safety of the moist, cool shelter. Star slipped in beside him. The stickytoes were already there. Click, Chirp, and Crunch squatted far back in the hollow trunk. The babes giggled as if they had played a silly trick once more. They waved and lovingly patted the stickytoes.

Above them, the forest creatures stampeded across the log toward the South Forest. Hooves and claws desperately sought footing among the dead tree's crooked limbs, which shot out at odd angles and prevented swift passage. Some of the creatures froze when they climbed on top of the log and looked down into the deep gorge. Shocked, they cowered in the branches on the log bridge—more afraid of falling into the depths of the gorge than of being burned by the approaching flames. Some simply crowded the north end of the log and refused to cross over once they saw the chasm, yet they were afraid to go back into the burning forest too.

Suddenly the cougar mum and her kits burst through the creatures blocking the route across the bridge, and deftly scrambled to the South Forest.

A thunderous roar echoed as a black bear shoved aside the blockade of frightened creatures, and with huge claws, tore the bark into pieces as it crossed. He left the trunk's bare wood exposed, slippery, and even more treacherous than before. The log bridge bounced, swayed, and finally cracked with the bear's mighty weight. Now afraid the log would collapse, the creatures ignored the dizzying height and raced madly across.

In growing despair, Leaf realized they had no way to cross the log. There were too many panicked creatures escaping to the South Forest. The Twig's only route was completely blocked. Leaf knew if they tried to cross, they would be knocked off and fall into the gorge. Warily, Leaf stood up and peeked out from the shadows.

The fire approached. Branches cracked and the eerie scream of the hot wind blasted the air above the log. Leaf shrank back and huddled against Star, terrified. The babes shivered in fear. The looksalot and stickytoes pressed their bodies into the moldy vines. Veil turned a deep shade of rotting, red bark. Leaf and Star tried to soothe the soft whimpers of the Twig babes and comfort

Veil, Crunch, Chirp, and Click. The damp, hollow trunk grew warmer and warmer. Smoke stung their eyes, and they began to choke.

Leaf could not help but watch from their shelter as frantic creatures scrambled for footing at the edge of the gorge. They teetered on its brink, off balance, scratching at the granite to keep from falling into the chasm.

Above them, debris fell from the log. Ripped up ferns, clumps of mud, torn moss, broken limbs, and shredded bark fell silently down toward the river. They were trapped! Very soon the smoke would suffocate them!

Oddly, from the depths of the cool, dark hollow where he crouched, Veil rolled his eyes in opposite directions. His scales turned brown. He rolled his eyes around once more then, with a strange, eerie stare, he focused both of them on Leaf.

CHAPTER TWENTY-FOUR

THE CROSSING
OF THE GUARD

Star put her arms around Veil in despair and moaned so quietly the babes could not hear. She whispered to Leaf, "How will we cross over? We'll be knocked from the log! If we stay," she choked on the words, "...the fire!"

In a sudden, deliberate, unexpected movement, Veil shook Star's arms from his neck, gradually uncurled his long green tail, and stepped in slow motion from the thick stick Leaf had struggled to pull deep into the ferns. He rocked back and forth to a long, jagged crack in the trunk. He crawled through the gap and disappeared.

Shocked, Leaf stuck his head through the gap, and searched for Veil. Not far away, the looksalot clung to the log *upside-down*. With a wide grin he unfurled his tail, and gripped a small branch that stuck out. He hung there, upside-down, rolled his eyes around, and again fixed them both on Leaf.

Instantly hopeful, Leaf looked at the route from the looksalot's view. Small limbs stuck out from underneath the log bridge and would easily give Veil hand and footholds all the way across to the South Forest. At once, Leaf cried out, "Star! The stickytoes and Veil can crawl across the log upside-down! They can carry the babes!"

Quickly, Star looked through the gap. She stared in disbelief at Veil who hung serenely from the bottom of the log bridge. Then she sat up next to Leaf. "Yes," she said slowly. "We will need to tie the babes to their carry-cradles very tight but it could be done."

Leaf motioned to Veil to return. With a stern look at Star, he stated flatly, "You must ride Veil across. You must go with the babes."

Ashamed suddenly, Star looked away. She knew Leaf was right. "Then we must make sure the ropes will hold the babes in their cradles," she said softly.

Leaf and Star hastily checked the babes' ropes. Next they pulled the ropes even tighter around the bellies of Chirp, Click, and Crunch. The stickytoes licked their eyes with their long, pink tongues, and pumped themselves up and down to test the hold of the ropes. Quickly, Leaf wrapped braided ropes around Veil's shoulders and belly for Star.

Worried and sad, Star turned and gazed at him hopelessly. "How will you get across?"

"Don't worry," Leaf said. "I won't be far behind you. I'll find a way."

Star nodded hopefully then climbed onto Veil's back. Leaf looped the rope over her shoulders and around her waist twice then back around Veil.

"All right, Leaf!" she finally exclaimed. "I'm tied tight enough!" She pressed his hand, and said firmly, "Stay right here. I'll send Veil back to carry you across. Just wait here."

Leaf could not look in her eyes. He doubted there would be enough time for Veil to return. "Hold on tight," he said fiercely. Then he called out to the babes, "Hold on really, really tight, dear babes! You're going to have a fantastically amazing ride to the South Forest! Now go!"

Sand, Moss, Breeze, Cone, and Mist giggled and waved to Leaf, excited by the strange upside-down ride on the stickytoes. Only Pool appeared pale and serious. He seemed to understand what they were about to do.

The stickytoes slipped through the gap in the log. Chirp took the lead and carefully tested each foothold. He grasped the upside-down limbs with great skill and even wrapped his long tongue around the thin branches to be sure they would hold. Crunch followed, then Click, then Veil. Very slowly . . . painfully slowly . . . they moved across the log bridge upside-down. Star tried not to look up at the sickening chasm. She concentrated on cheering on the babes, who giggled with every step the stickytoes took. They waved their tiny stick arms freely below their heads and shouted to Star, "Look at me! Look at me!" Even Pool smiled.

Leaf grinned in spite of how much fear he felt.

Now the thick smoke curled and fell over the edge of the canyon wall not from Leaf. He peeked above the ferns covering the cave. Even more forest creatures flooded across the log bridge now. With an ugly grunt, a bristling, mean wolverine shoved the smaller creatures aside, and bullied its way across. Smoke drifted through the air and a hot wind sucked Leaf's breath away.

Far across from where Leaf huddled, Pappo, Moon, Sapper, Ruffle, and Tuffle perched halfway up a tree and kept watch on the terrible flood of creatures scrambling across the log. They were sure Leaf, Star, and the babes must be trying to cross too. The smoke flowed in lumpy drifts to their side of the gorge. Their eyes stung and watered. The Cappynut Twigs generously shared their feathers with Pappo and Moon. All of them waved the feathers under their noses to clear the air. They watched the log intently, hoping against hope to spot the Twigs escaping south.

Moon saw them first. He spotted the stickytoes and looksalot creeping along slowly under the log. Click, Chirp, Crunch, and Veil clung securely and almost peacefully underneath the massive bridge. The babes waved at Moon happily. Moon tugged at Pappo's arm and pointed at the strange group making their way across. "Look! There! They're coming across underneath the log!"

"But where's Leaf?" Pappo cried out at once. "Do you see Leaf with them?"

Moon slid over the mossy rocks and crouched as near the edge as he dared. He searched anxiously for Leaf. Finally, he only shook his head. Pappo checked with

Sapper and the twins who had searched for Leaf, too. They shook their heads. None saw Leaf.

On the north rim, the fire grew closer to the edge of the gorge. It encircled the log bridge's topmost branches which had been held in place for many long seasons by the boulders. A high, brittle limb from the sugar pine snapped, was swept up in the sucking wind, caught fire, and violently burst apart on the middle of the bridge. The creatures on the south side of the exploding branch raced hastily across to the lush green South Forest. The creatures on the north side were blocked and forced back. They stumbled blindly into the suffocating smoke. Those now safe in the South Forest paused in its damp green ferns, and stared back, astonished at their lucky escape.

Crackling, red flames whipped the tree's bark and now scorched the trunk of the log bridge. The branch had exploded just above where the stickytoes and Veil crawled underneath.

But in slow-motion, the odd-looking rescuers continued to make their way to the South Forest. The stickytoes clutched the bark, focused only on each movement. They struggled to find the strongest hold, ever mindful of the giggling Twig babes on their backs. Veil grasped the ancient tree's bark with his two-toed hands and feet, steady and sure. He followed the stickytoes closely, rolling his eyes, and ever ready to catch a falling babe with his far-reaching tongue.

Grimly, Star looked back to where Leaf waited in the vines. Smoke and ashes fell on each side of the log bridge, and blocked her view.

The flaming branch which had fallen on the log bridge now set the entire tree on fire. It raced back and forth on top of the trunk, crackling furiously as it burned the dry timber. Soon it snaked around and burned along the bottom of the log too.

Star looked back again and searched for Leaf through the thick, curling smoke that fell from the top of the log into the terrifying abyss below. Her tears cooled her face.

"Leaf! Leaf!" Pappo screamed and stretched on tiptoe, searching through the flames and smoke for his son. "I don't see him! I can't see him! Leaf!" Pappo choked on the smoke.

Moon, Sapper, and the twins looked at each other sadly, and shook their heads.

CHAPTER TWENTY-FIVE

BARKBITERS FLEE

Moon paced back and forth. He motioned frantically to the stickytoes and looksalot to hurry. He screamed at them, "Don't look behind you!" He grew sick as he watched the flames spread and come closer to Star and the babes. He knelt in the moss and begged the stickytoes and Veil to crawl faster, faster!.

But Star saw they would now make it safely across. They were very near the south edge. Click, Chirp, and Crunch continued to place one careful hand and foothold after the other, ensuring each exacting grasp held tight before moving the other foot or hand. The looksalot followed just as methodically, tail wrapped into a flat swirl for better balance. Star's arms were wrapped around Veil's neck in a viselike grip.

Moon was in agony. He shouted and waved at them to move faster!

In the middle of the log, a golden noose of fire began to choke the ancient bridge. Blazing red fingers clutched the bark beneath the log and scratched their way toward Star and the babes. The stickytoes and looksalot seemed to creep in slow motion through the falling smoke. Finally, Chirp's nose touched the soft moss clinging to the edge of the south gorge. The stickytoes scrambled up the embankment quickly followed by Veil.

Joyfully, Moon embraced each tiny Twig babe and then, finally, Star. He dragged them all back away from the treacherous cliff and burning log. Pappo, Moon, and the Cappynut Twigs carried the babes and Star deep into the safety of the green forest and left them in a small, abandoned fox den. The stickytoes and the looksalot rapidly climbed into the overhanging low branches. Veil's tail drooped. He no longer had the strength to curl it. Exhausted, the stickytoes and looksalot watched the horrific scene unfold across the wide gap.

Leaf could not be seen anywhere. Moon, Pappo, Ruffle, and Tuffle hopped along the edge of the gorge and peered through the drifting smoke, searching for any sign of Leaf. Finally Pappo spotted his son's slight figure through swirling ash. Leaf was scrambling up one of the sugar pine trees.

At that same moment, Moon started screaming, "Barkbiters! Barkbiters!"

Hundreds of scrabbling, black barkbiters poured from the smoke-filled forest. They spilled over the cliff in a dark waterfall of prickly legs and clicking pinchers. Their red eyes glared and their wings beat against the smoke in a hopeless flurry. They could only crawl or float in the air, not fly, so they plunged over the cliff, and dropped far down into the powerfully swift river. Their stubby wings could not save them in the raging rapids.

Many barkbiters tried to scratch their way across the log, but they were sucked into the flames. More barkbiters trampled those scrambling to crawl back from the burning bridge. At the edge of the chasm, a tower of barkbiters grew thicker and higher until finally it simply toppled over. The black tower plummeted down, an ugly mass that spiraled silently to the river below.

Some barkbiters scratched at the granite cliff face and tried to climb backwards down the canyon walls, but their heavy, clumsy bodies could not hold their own weight so they fell, belly up. Their legs curled up then frantically clawed at the air as they spun into the chasm.

In anguish, Pappo watched as ugly red-eyed barkbiters poured from the curling smoke by the hundreds. They crowded into any place not touched by the fire. Pappo watched in horror as the barkbiters crawled up the sugar pine where Leaf climbed—dangerously higher and higher. Terrified, Pappo watched the gruesome barkbiters creep nearer and nearer to his son. Leaf was trapped!

Across from Pappo, in the midst of the hot ash, Leaf heard a *WHIZZ! WHIZZ!* and then a terrific *WHACK!* as a small rock bounced off of the limb right below his feet. He instinctively ducked as another rock whizzed by his nose. Just then, a whistling stone barely missed Leaf's head but a barkbiter was brutally whacked off a nearby branch. The ugly, evil bug exploded into pieces. More and more barkbiters were struck by whizzing rocks. *WHIZZ! WHIZZ! WHACK!*

Across the gorge, Leaf saw three blue- and yellow-feathered Twigs running back and forth along the south cliff edge. They wielded their slingers with deadly precision. The round pebbles whizzed across the canyon at the barkbiters. Leaf waved to the Cappynut Twigs excitedly. Ruffle, Tuffle, and Sapper loaded and shot their slingers as quickly as they could grab the stones from the ground. *Ping! Ping! Crunch!* The barkbiters were hit, crushed, and their fat bodies ripped apart as they were knocked dead from the limbs.

But now Leaf had to dodge the rocks, too. The barkbiters were outpacing the rocks even though the Cappynuts were fast and deadly with their aim.

Leaf climbed higher. Quickly, he fashioned a loop with his rope. Desperately, he threw it to a nearby tree, but the loop snagged on a thin branch. Leaf knew at once the branch could not hold his weight so he jumped wildly toward the tree and crashed into the dry branches. Bruised but safe for the time being, he waved to Pappo.

Far below, Leaf saw the barkbiters now swarming the roots of the tree where he perched. Leaf wondered if perhaps he could swing on his rope to another tree. He tugged frantically to free his rope, but it would not tear loose. He knew he was too high above the ground to jump over the barkbiters. Soon the flames would reach them all anyway.

Leaf looked in despair across the chasm. The Cappynut Twigs were flinging two stones at a time now at the barkbiters, but soon Leaf knew they would have no strength left to sling their rocks so far. Pappo and Moon ran back and forth throwing rocks across the gorge. But their rocks fell far short.

At last, Leaf knew there would be no help against the never-ending onslaught of barkbiters or the firestorm. Relentlessly, the biters crawled up even as the choking smoke curled in the branches. Even so, Leaf climbed higher. Soon he clung to a skinny limb at the very tip of the immense sugar pine tree. He looked down at the smoke swirling below. Flames shot up from shorter trees nearby and whipped their branches into ash. Gold fingers of fire now stretched greedily below him, racing up the tree's trunk. The flames forced the barkbiters to scratch toward him faster and nearer.

Through the smoke Leaf could see the slender figure of Star standing at the rim's edge. She stood as still as granite, her hands clasped together, and watched in horror.

Tears stung Leaf's eyes. There were no more limbs to climb. No place else to go!

CHAPTER TWENTY-SIX

WHO CAN SAVE A TWIG?

A black shadow swept over Leaf. Dark wings flapped just above him. Thin, sharp claws clutched at his leafy head. Leaf ducked down just as a stiff wing whacked his face. A shrill whistle cut the air! It was Pesky!

Pesky spun in a circle and stretched his claws out toward Leaf. Still, Leaf ducked down. The tooler's claws looked sharper than an eagle's. In despair, Leaf stared down at the barkbiters crawling up the sugar pine's trunk. Their red eyes burned hotter than the fire. He looked up at Pesky's claws. The tooler's wings brushed his leafy hair, and Pesky circled even closer to his head. For just an instant, Pesky dipped his wing towards Leaf.

Immediately, Leaf knew what he must do. He held his breath, closed his eyes, and flung himself through the air. His fingers slid through Pesky's ash-filled feathers but Leaf managed to grasp hold of two. He opened his eyes and realized he was gripping Pesky's tail! It flipped up and down as Pesky banked into a steep dive. Leaf closed his eyes again and concentrated on keeping his fists clinched. His feet dangled behind Pesky wildly as they were both swept up in the hot wind.

At last Leaf caught a breath of cool air. He sneezed. His leafy head was now full of ash, too. Cautiously, Leaf opened his eyes. He was shocked.

Below, the burning log collapsed into the deep chasm. It fell away in great, fiery, burning chunks. At the same time, Leaf thought he saw black water flowing into the cliff, but at once he realized it was a waterfall of bark-biters spilling over the north rim. Wave after wave fell into the deep gorge. The fireball behind them suddenly roared furiously. Leaf gasped, gripped Pesky's feathers tighter, and closed his eyes.

Sweet, green, fragrant ferns rushed at Leaf's face and whipped his leafy hair into tangles. Pesky skidded into deep, moist moss and glossy-leafed bushes. Leaf sucked in cool air and let go of the tooler's tail feathers. He swirled around in circles, slid on wet moss, and ended up in a mud bank near a creek. Leaf opened his eyes. He sat covered in sticky, brown slime but he was finally safe. His eyes blinked happily through the mud on his face.

Pappo lifted Leaf up from the mud and hugged him— or, rather, crushed him—laughing, and relieved his son was now safe.

Suddenly Leaf was in the middle of a mob of skinny, stick arms squeezing him tightly. Jubilant shouts rang in his ears. Star, Moon, the Cappynut Twigs, and the Twig babes hooted and danced around him, celebrating his rescue. They even hugged and kissed Pesky until he had enough. With a clumsy hop and a brisk flutter he broke free, flew to a nearby branch, and sat frowning down at them.

Leaf stood in the middle of all of their smiling faces, looked up at the disgruntled Pesky, and shouted, "Pesky, you are the most wonderful tooler in the forest!"

Pesky fluffed up his feathers, shook ashes from his wings, and whistled a bright, strident "*thank you very much*" to Leaf. Then he lifted his beak at a very snobby tilt, sprung from the branch, and flew away, as far away from the fire and smoke as he could fly.

CHAPTER TWENTY-SEVEN

TWIGS ON GUARD

The next morning, the sun shimmered through a crimson haze. The Cappynut Twigs sat in the cold, damp moss, and preened their blue and yellow feathers. They rubbed them with dewdrops to try and rid each thin wispy strand of the smell of smoke. Ruffle and Tuffle cast curious, wide eyes at Star but shyly looked away whenever she turned to smile at them.

Star soaked packs of moss and rubbed the stickytoes' orange-spotted skin to moisten it to a shiny reflection.

Veil sat on a low branch, winding and unwinding his long tail with a mysterious, wide grin on his face. Not far away from Veil, a small, bluish looksalot with rolling, turquoise eyes and soft, delicate two-toed feet hid in the leaves. Veil and the blue looksalot rolled their eyes all around, yet one eye always seemed to focus on each other. Finally, painfully slowly, Veil stepped along his branch and politely squatted closer to her. After a while, Veil and the pretty blue looksalot curled their very long tails together and sat grinning.

Moon and Star watched the smitten looksalots and knew Veil had found a mate for life.

Near where the Twigs sheltered, many forest creatures lay exhausted. All night, the creatures and beasts hid in the thick undergrowth while flames shot into the night sky across the gorge. None of them had attacked or even threatened one another as they huddled, frightened. They had lain side by side but now, as the dawn lit the day, they recovered their old fears. Once again they felt threatened. Their animosities returned. Their suspicions grew. Stealthily, they crept, slithered, crawled, padded, or flew away from each other.

Moon watched them leave and felt sad. Soon only the Twigs clustered in the tangled roots of an enormous cedar tree. The stickytoes were constantly swabbed down by Star with wet moss, as if the smell of ash were permanent. Silently, Leaf stared across the gorge at the burnt trees and thin drifting smoke. He was struck speechless by the devastating waste.

Leaf thought of the colorful, flowing bands of the Dancing Sky Lights they had watched last night. They had appeared even brighter and stronger than the leaping fire. It was an incredible sight. Bathed in their beauty and strange, mysterious patterns, Pappo and Sapper lay on their backs and watched the mesmerizing display. Now worn out, the two older Twigs nodded their drowsy heads, and lay slumped among the roots.

Forgetting yesterday's danger, Sand, Pool, Moss, Breeze, Cone, and Mist happily dug shallow hollows on the bank of the nearby stream and covered their arms and legs with mud.

"Look at us, Star!" they shouted cheerfully. Pretending to be Leaf, they had patted mud all over their faces. Their eyes blinked brightly through the brown slime. "Betcha' can't see us!" they giggled.

Finally, the stickytoes decided to escape Star's prolonged wet-down. Click, Crunch, and Chirp scampered up a nearby tree and squatted on a fat branch, still dripping, but well hidden against the red bark, in case Star tried to find them.

Star sighed. She walked to the creek bank to wipe the mud from the babes' faces. They were giggling so much she hesitated. With a grin, she plopped down in the muddy hollow with them and, to their delight, covered her own face and hands with mud. Leaf watched them play happily in the sparkling creek.

Later, Star cleaned the sleepy babes up and handed out plump, juicy berries, and sips of water. At last the tiny babes lay quiet and napped.

Leaf pulled Star away from her vigilant watch over the babes and forced her to sit on the moss beside him and rest.

"We're all right now, Star. Rest a while." Leaf nodded at Moon, who sat nearby and watched the babes sleep. His face had an odd, sweet, loving expression. "Moon and I will care for the babes," Leaf said patiently. "You will need your strength for the trip to your new haven, the Old Seeder."

Moon turned abruptly and interrupted Leaf, his voice defiant, "We can't leave here."

Leaf looked at him irritably.

Ruffle and Tuffle paused grooming their feathers and glanced at Moon, surprised at his defiant tone of voice.

Moon stood up, placed his hands on his hips, and stared at Leaf. With a no-nonsense frown, he explained, "Not all the barkbiters died, that's for sure. We have to stay here and make sure none of them ever cross over to the South Forest."

Leaf appeared bewildered for a moment. "But we saw them fall into the gorge. . . . They burned in the fire. . . . " his words faded as he realized that Moon was probably right. Some biters may have escaped.

Ruffle and Tuffle scrambled to their feet. They threw their skinny arms over each other's shoulders, and declared to Moon in unison, "We'll stay with you! We'll keep those barkbiters away from our forest! We stick together 'cause we're Twigs!" Then they both shyly glanced at Star, hoping she noticed how brave they were to join Moon in the gorge watch.

Sapper roused himself from the roots at the sound of their voices. He now joined in. "Don't worry, Star," he said. "We're excellent hunters. No barkbiters will dare cross over as long as we have our slingers. Other Twigs live near the gorge. The Canyon Twigs! They'll help, too! We'll be Gorge Guards!"

Ruffle and Tuffle cried out, "No barkbiters will pass this way! We have our slingers!" Their eyes shone hopefully. Perhaps Star already knew how skillful they could be with slingers.

Actually she did realize it, and she did notice them. "That's wonderful of you," she praised them both with a sweet, sincere smile.

Ruffle and Tuffle winked at one another, loaded their slingers with pebbles, took aim at pine cones high in the pine trees, and swiftly whacked them off the branches.

Sapper rolled his eyes. "Show offs!" he muttered to Pappo.

Pappo answered flatly, "Like we were any different?" The two friends laughed, remembering when they were also shy and awkward.

Star looked around the pretty sunlit glade where they sheltered from the fire and added, "This spot is a wonderful place to live. The trees here are beautiful. There's plenty of food and water. Look," she said, "the babes have already decided this is home."

Star pointed to the cluster of babe heads. Their buds were just beginning to uncurl in the sun. Their leafy hair took on various shades of green, gold, and silver. Pool and Breeze were actually playing together nicely for once. They patted muddy creature shapes along the bank and leaned their heads in close as they seriously discussed the important aspects of creature shaping. Sand sat nearby, pointing at the shapes and adding her critical comments. Moss, Cone, and Mist rolled a smooth river stone from the top of the bank to the bottom, and raced along beside as it splashed into the shallow creek.

Star turned back to Ruffle, Tuffle, Moon, and Leaf, and with a glow on her face, said, "We're home at last. This is our haven now."

CHAPTER TWENTY-EIGHT

FARE WELL

As Leaf watched the babes play, he realized he had not seen Pesky since his rescue the evening before. He wondered where the brave tooler had flown, so he looked at the treetops and around the pretty meadow. Just as he caught Star's eye to ask if she had seen Pesky, a harsh, thumping beat of wings filled the air above them. They threw their hands up in defense at the sudden onslaught. Star and Leaf cringed. They peeked through their arms then they heard a bright, cheery whistle!

Pesky slid to a clumsy halt in the clearing. Before Leaf or Star could utter a word, a frail, old Twig, slid from his back. It was Mook! Pesky had flown to fetch him from the Old Seeder. No one could tell if Mook shook from weakness or from excitement as he trembled, and grinned at them all.

"PapaMook!" cried out Star and Moon at the same instant, and rushed into his arms.

"PapaMook! PapaMook!" screamed the delighted babes. They rushed over, still wet and muddy from the creek bank. Breeze and Cone clung to his skinny legs. Moss, Pool, and Mist tugged at his elbows. Sand simply jumped in a circle around him, clapping her hands with joy.

Pappo stepped over to embrace the old Twig. "Mook!" cried out Pappo. "They're all safe, see, like I told you! Here they are! All safe!" Pappo stepped back and grinned at the loving mob of tangled up Twigs.

Eventually, Mook fell over backwards from the crush of happiness. Star began pulling off the babes in alarm. Moon pulled back the tiny Twig bodies and admonished them. "Enough! Enough now! Breeze, Mist, Cone, Sand, Pool, and Moss! You sit in a circle now. Sit around PapaMook now! Stop crushing him!" The babes calmed down and sat as Moon had asked.

Star and Moon held Mook's hands and sat down crossed-legged beside him. Mook sat quietly. Joyful tears streamed down his face over a huge, shining smile.

In a weak, squeaky voice, he said, "Thank you! Thank you, Needles, Leaf, Whisper, Sapper, Ruffle, and Tuffle! Thank you, Star and Moon, for keeping the babes safe! I can't tell you how grateful I am!"

Whisper wriggled her ears at the sound of her name. The sweet, spotted chipmunk realized the old Twig was crying. She stepped gently over the babes and nuzzled Mook's leafy, white head to comfort him. The loving gesture brought another outburst of giggles from the babes. Whisper's eyes twinkled and her whiskers twitched.

Pesky hopped up to the nearest low-hanging branch, and preened the dust from his feathers. He tilted his head to one side, and glared at the noisy Twig mob's celebration.

Mook disentangled his hand from Moon's and waved to the standoffish tooler. "Thank you, too, Pesky! We would never be here without you!" The praise drew clapping and cheers from the Twigs. Pesky very nearly bowed to the applause, then, snobby once more, searched for worms.

"PapaMook," Star said as the merry voices finally quieted. "We're going to live here if it's all right with you. The Cappynut Twigs are staying with us to make our new haven safe and guard the gorge from the bark-biters." Star looked gratefully at Ruffle and Tuffle.

The twins grinned so broadly they almost looked as if they were in pain.

Star continued, "The Cappynuts will be guards for the South Forest. And there are other Twigs who live nearby, and they will help too."

Mook's hands slowly stopped trembling. He was finally reassured they were all safe at last. Still unsteady, however, he stood up on wobbly legs and wordlessly motioned to Leaf. Surprised, Leaf stepped over immediately to prevent the old Twig from falling over.

"My dear Leaf," Mook placed his hand on Leaf's shoulder, "I owe you everything. If you had not flown off right away, who knows if the barkbiters might have found the cave first? Because of your bravery, you brought my family safely back to me!" Mook hugged the young Twig.

Leaf protested, "Oh, no." He felt awkward and too embarrassed to mention he didn't really know how dangerous it was when he left the Old Seeder. He muttered, "It was Pesky that saved us! And Star and Moon were the brave ones! And Pappo and the Cappynuts! Leaf paused, caught his breath then added, "And Whisper!"

Whisper fluffed up her fur, groomed her bristly tail, and acted as if being praised meant nothing to her. But her sweet eyes glimmered under long brown eyelashes as she blinked at Leaf. Then she nudged her way over, gently pushed Mook away, and nuzzled Leaf's emerald, leafy head to show him how happy she was that he was now safe. Leaf threw his skinny brown arms around her neck and kissed her speckled cheeks.

"Pappo," Leaf suddenly asked, "can we stay and guard the gorge too?"

Pappo stroked his chin as he thought it over. "Well, I think we should definitely stay here for a while. But soon we'll need to go home and tell Mumma, Fern, Buddy, and Burba what we're up to, don't you think? I imagine they'll love to hear about this adventure!"

Leaf nodded, accepting Pappo's decision. "Yes, but maybe they'll want to come back and see the great chasm for themselves!"

Pappo laughed and slapped his knees. "You're right!" he agreed. "Now, we need to find a great tree haven for our new North Twig neighbors," Pappo directed briskly. "Let's find the biggest and best knothole we can!"

The babes cried out at the prospect of finding a tree to call home. Immediately they scrambled up the largest trees, seeking a roomy knothole.

Star and Moon ran off to gather them up and lead them in some order to search for a home. They wandered around in the sunlit clearing, looking up and examining the giant trunks.

Veil and his new, bluish-colored looksalot mate swayed in slow rhythm. Star had quickly named her Sky for her blue scales. Sky and Veil rolled their eyes at all the activity, and climbed higher into the branches. They'd rather smack bugs together. They took turns whipping out their extraordinary long tongues and admiring each other's munching techniques. Obviously they wished to be left out of the haven hunt.

Crunch, Click, and Chirp scurried around, poking their noses into every hole in every trunk around the clearing. They swished their long, shiny tails back and forth excitedly. Chirp investigated deep knotholes by climbing down as far as he could and hanging onto the edge with his tail. He busily pushed dead leaves and panicked bugs from their shadowy depths to get a good view. Crunch and Click waited patiently nearby and greedily snatched up the bugs as they flew or crawled out while trying to escape.

At last, Moon spotted a huge, protruding knothole halfway up a tall prehistoric cedar tree. After exploring it completely, Moon poked his head out and shouted to the expectant group below, "It's perfect for us!"

Delighted, the babes and Star scrambled up at once to inspect their new haven. Pappo and Sapper followed, carefully guiding and assisting Mook as he painstakingly worked his way up to the knothole.

Leaf, Ruffle, and Tuffle gathered soft ferns and moss for beds and blankets. After stuffing the knothole with all sorts of useful items, the young Twigs collected seeds, nuts, and berries for their food stores. At last, after much scurrying about and busy activity, the knothole was deemed a worthy haven for the North Twig family.

Finally the Twig babes lay on soft moss beds in the inner hollow of the mammoth trunk. Sound asleep, they snored peacefully, lulled into dreams by the soft brush of cedar fronds all around their haven. Even the blue jays quieted their noisy chatter and napped on nearby limbs.

The Cappynut Twigs wasted no time seeking help to guard the South Forest from an attack by the dreadful barkbiters. Sapper, Ruffle, and Tuffle set off to find the brave and valiant Canyon Twigs who lived along the south edge of the great chasm. The Canyon Twigs would be delighted to learn all about their new neighbors—Star, Moon, Mook, and the babes. Pappo tagged along to renew old friendships and meet any new Twigs who may have moved into this part of the forest.

Moon wanted to stay and take care of the babes. Star was surprised, but grateful, for his new feeling of responsibility.

Leaf and Star sat quietly on a branch outside her new haven's knothole and gazed across the gorge at the devastated North Forest. "It's so sad," Leaf blurted out. "Your home is gone."

Star simply nodded and glanced at Leaf. "I only think about today . . . and tomorrow." She sighed. "Your forest is beautiful, Leaf," she added.

"It's yours now, Star," Leaf said. "You and Mook and Moon and the babes will be happy here, I'm sure." Leaf swung his legs off the side of the limb and smiled at Star. "Wait 'til you come visit my haven! It's the tallest tree in the forest! We call it the Old Seeder."

"Oh, I bet it's wonderful!" Star's eyes brightened. "Is it so tall that we could climb up to the top and see . . . everything?"

"Sure." Leaf grinned proudly. He looked up and nodded toward the very highest limbs swaying far above them. A light breeze tickled the topmost fronds and framed them against the bright, blue sky. "The Old Seeder is so tall that I bet we can even see it from up there!" Leaf pointed skyward.

"You wanna bet?" asked Star, taking up the challenge.

"Let's see!" Leaf scrambled to his feet and began climbing as fast as his hands could grasp the limbs above his head. Star laughed and swiftly climbed up the other side of the massive, red trunk. Finally they reached the highest branches. Star and Leaf clung to the slender, bouncing limbs and breathed in the sweet smell of sticky cedar sap. The sharp, cool breeze softly kissed their faces.

"There it is!" Leaf proudly pointed to a far away emerald tip of the ancient cedar which rose majestically above wavering wisps of clouds. The Old Seeder was a giant in the vast forest. No other tree grew so tall. Along the dark green edge of the South Forest ran the sapphire-colored Sharp Peaks, a jagged border braced against a stark, cloudless, blue sky.

Yet even more startling than the Sharp Peaks, stood the lone, white mountain which towered behind the

Old Seeder—Echo Peak. Smothering its massive, high mountain tip was the brilliant, crystalline glacier called the Long Ice.

"It's amazing!" Star gasped, awestruck.

"That's my home!" Leaf declared proudly. They gazed at the unbelievable view for a long while.

A cool breeze gently stirred the pale green fronds around them like dandelion fluff when a soft breath blew them apart.

Star and Leaf swayed peacefully on the thin limb, and talked about the beauty of the South Forest. After a while, they looked back across the immense chasm at the scorched North Forest. Their feeling of contentment was replaced by tremendous sorrow. They fell silent.

Then Leaf pointed above the tree tops which looked like smoldering skeletons in the black ash. "Look, Star!" he cried out suddenly. "The birds are already returning to your forest!"

Star gazed in astonishment as the shimmering wings of many differently colored birds soared around the burnt treetops. They dipped their wings, floated down, and somehow found a safe, cool spot to land among the devastation. They dropped out of sight into the smoking trees.

Leaf and Star looked at each other in surprise.

"Do you think the forest will ever be the same?" Star asked Leaf hopefully. "Without the barkbiters, I mean."

Leaf stared at the gray, ashy landscape across the chasm and answered softly, "No, probably not just the same."

Star dropped her eyes in disappointment and blinked to hold back her stinging tears.

Leaf continued, his voice kind, "But green again, Star, I'm sure. Maybe all the barkbiters burned up, and the trees will have a chance to grow green and strong again. Maybe," he paused, trying to find the right words, "maybe the fire was a good thing." He looked at Star reassuringly.

Star gazed at the vast expanse of charred trees. She wondered if, after all, the fire was a good thing. Thoughtfully, she murmured, "The trees hated the bark-biters, too, you know."

"Look!" Leaf suddenly pointed at a heavy, smoky cloud lingering over the North Forest.

Star held her hand above her eyes to block the sun, squinted, and looked to where Leaf pointed. She saw nothing but wisps of swirling ash caught in the restless breeze. Still, she searched the spot intently where Leaf stubbornly pointed. Finally she gave up, shook her silvery, leafy head, and frowned at Leaf. "I don't see anything. What do you see?"

"Look!" Leaf urged her. He cradled her chin and turned her face toward a distant ridge. "Look, again, Star. Just there! Look!"

Star peered into the drifting, low cloud but whatever it smothered was well hidden so she scanned the steep ridge rising above the gray haze.

Just then a slight flash of white feathers sparkled high above the mist as a large bird shook the ash from its wings.

Star spotted the yellow, hooked beak of a great hunter. It was a striking, deadly silhouette against the blue sky. On a tall tree which somehow escaped the flames, an eagle clung to a fragile limb, swayed, and stared at the forest floor. Star followed the eagle's steady, piercing gaze and wondered what had moved that captured its interest so intensely.

It was then she saw it.

A huge, lumbering beast, a spirit bear with white, golden-tipped fur, trudged north through the charred trees of the burned forest.

Following along behind her broad swaying back were three spirit bear cubs, covered in ash, gleefully pouncing on heaping, cool piles of cinders. They rolled over and over in the soft, gray dust, batted smoke-colored puff-balls floating in the air, sneezed, and joyfully pounced again.

With tears in her eyes, Star smiled.

Bark beetles are real.
They attack and destroy millions of trees
and entire forests.
Many believe global warming is causing
this horrifying epidemic
and there is no way to stop it.
But there are brave guardians
who protect our trees
and battle bark beetles.
Many are in organizations
sworn to defend our forests.
Please support their efforts.
Please save our trees.

Leaf & the Rushing Waters

A massive landslide pushes a river off course and at once, it surrounds Leaf's ancient tree home! Desperate to save the Old Seeder, Leaf seeks proud, goliath beavers to help build a dam and block the brutal river. But who'll help Leaf, his friends, and their jittery chipmunks as owls, foxes, and rattlesnakes stalk them! And what about the hornets? Who will save the Old Seeder?

Leaf & the Long Ice

Excited by stories of snow, Leaf's twin brothers, Buddy and Burba, ride a giant moth to the perilous shrinking glacier of Echo Peak! Unaware of the danger, they befriend a bunny and a mountain goat kid. At once, a cruel fox pursues them into a deadly ice tunnel maze. A bewildered Leaf, a heroic mouse, and a scary hermit, are the only hope for the Twig twins!

Leaf & Echo Peak

Rumblings in Echo Peak foreshadow an eruption! Twigs must escape when the volcano wakes up, but all the forest paths are precarious. Many follow Leaf and courageous marmots down into a prehistoric lava tube but vicious bats and creepy moles block their way! Where can Twigs hide when a volcano erupts?

ABOUT THE AUTHOR

Jo Marshall is the author of the Twig adventures *Leaf & the Sky of Fire, Leaf & the Rushing Waters, Leaf & the Long Ice,* and *Leaf & Echo Peak.* She lives in sight of the volcanic Cascade mountains and the prehistoric rainforests of the Pacific Northwest. Twig stories are inspired by the climate changes affecting the region's active volcanoes, their shrinking glaciers, vanishing old growth forests, and the impact on native wildlife. Jo is a member of the Society of Environmental Journalists, the Society of Children's Book Writers and Illustrators, and numerous nonprofit groups which advocate for nature conservancy, protection of endangered wildlife, and finding solutions to global warming. During her stint as a career military family member, Jo earned a B.A. in German Language and Literature while living in West Berlin. Presently, she resides in Snohomish, Washington with her husband, son, daughter, and many loving creatures.

ABOUT THE ARTIST

D.W. MURRAY is an award-winning Disney and Universal Pictures artist whose screen credits include *Mulan*, *Tarzan*, *Lilo & Stitch*, *Brother Bear*, and *Curious George*. An award recipient of the prestigious New York Society of Illustrators Gallery, his talent is also recognized by the 2004 Gold Aurora Award. He has written numerous screenplays, pitched story concepts to Roy Disney, and to the producers of *Touched By An Angel*. D.W. Murray is the author of the fantasy novels, *Majesty -The Sorcerer and the Saint* and *Majesty and the Dragon's Throne* which are compared to the Chronicles of Narnia. He is a former scriptwriter for *Big Ideas* and the colorful children's animated series *3-2-1 Penguins*. He resides with his family in Florida. More about D.W. Murray is on his website, www.dwmurraybooks.com.

www.twigstories.com

8138231R0

Made in the USA
Charleston, SC
11 May 2011